SCREAMER

SOULLESS KINGS MC: MARBLE FALLS, TX
BOOK 5

ANDI RHODES

BLUE JOURNEY PUBLISHING

Copyright © 2025 by Andi Rhodes

All rights reserved.

No part of this book may be reproduced in any form or by any electronic or mechanical means, including information storage and retrieval systems, without written permission from the author, except for the use of brief quotations in a book review.

This is a work of fiction and the product of the author's imagination. All names, characters, businesses, places, events and incidents are used in a fictitious manner, unless otherwise noted. Any resemblance to actual persons, living or deceased, or actual events is purely coincidental.

Cover Artwork - © Dez Purington at Pretty in Ink Creations

Editing - Darcie Fisher at Into the Gray Author Services

A NOTE FROM THE AUTHOR:

Welcome back to the world of the Soulless Kings MC: Marble Falls, TX chapter! This is Screamer and Roxie's story, and it's also the very last book of the series and of the Soulless Kings MC world (I really mean it this time lol).

Screamer and Roxie come from similar worlds, and they each have their own traumatic experiences to overcome. For some, their story may be triggering, but rest assured, they get their HEA!

I want to also take a moment to thank all of you, my readers, who have gone on the incredible journey this world took us. It's been so much fun, and I'm going to miss the SKMC family more than I care to admit. That being said, I've got many more bikers kicking around in my head and can't wait to share them with you!

Now, kick back with your favorite beverage and enjoy!

Much love,

Andi

For all my Soulless Kings fans… Without you, this world wouldn't be possible. Thank you for loving these characters as much as I do!

Screamer...

My life began the moment I patched in with the Soulless Kings MC. I left all the pain and heartache of my existence behind when I became part of that family, and nothing can make me look at the past or examine the events that scarred my soul... Or so I thought.

When *she* enters my world, I can tell she's built from the same cloth as me. The problem is, her scars also cause the fear she tries so hard to hide. Patience has never been a virtue of mine, but Roxie's testing me in ways that force me to dig deeper than I've ever had to before.

Roxie...

I left Marble Falls for a reason, left the only life I knew to see what else was out there, and all I got for my trouble were bruises and scars that only those who care to look can see. So, I came home, returning to the one place on the planet where I feel a modicum of safety, especially with my brother's motorcycle club at my back.

Trust doesn't come easy for me, especially when it comes to my heart and my Harley, but I'm told that *he* is someone who can help with the latter. Little by little, Screamer uncovers my secrets and teaches me that not all men are horrible, and before I know it, he's the one person who makes me want things I thought were long since impossible.

PROLOGUE
SCREAMER

I FOUND MY PEOPLE THAT NIGHT, ALONG WITH MY PURPOSE.

Eighteen years old...

"Where will you go?"

I stare at the manila envelope in my hand, the lawyer's question going in one ear and out the other. The last few weeks have been a nightmare that I'd give anything to wake up from, but that's not an option because I'm wide fucking awake.

"Don't know," I say with a shrug. "As far away from here as I can get."

He nods as if he understands, but he can't possibly fathom what I'm going through. He sits here in his cushy office, surrounded by pictures of his wife and kids, and content in the knowledge that he has people to go home to. As for me, I've got no one. Not anymore. Not after the night my entire life changed.

"Well, when you do settle down somewhere, call with your address so I can get you the rest of the estate."

"Estate?" I scoff. "My family hardly had enough for rent, let alone an *estate*."

"That's true," he says. "But Ally had a life insurance policy, as well as her marital home, several cars, and bank acc—"

"I don't give a shit about any of that," I snarl.

"Be that as it may, with the death of Ally and your parents, and the incarceration of Ally's husband, it all comes to you."

A vice squeezes my heart, and my eyes burn with tears I refuse to shed. Ally, my big sister, was murdered by her husband, and when he was done with her, he took out our parents, too. The only reason I'm still breathing is because I ran to the store to get condoms for my date the next day.

I'm the only living member of my family because my anger and dick were making decisions for me.

"Fine," I mutter, rising from the chair. "Are we done here?"

I have to get out of this stuffy office. I need a ride

and fresh air before I lose my shit and fall so far down into the void that I can never recover.

"We are. And again, I'm sorry for your loss."

Storming out of the office, I make my way to the ground floor of the building. I take the steps to try and burn off some of this rage, but it doesn't help. If anything, the second I step outside, all I want to do is lie down and die.

I climb on my Harley and race as fast as I can away from this town, from the pain and memories. I don't have a destination in mind and figure I'll know it when I get there.

Two months later, I roll into a little town called Marble Falls in Texas. I've been aimlessly traveling the country, using some of the money I got from my sister's estate, but I'm tired. So. Fucking. Tired.

The first thing I see when I turn onto Main Street is a motorcycle parked in front of a building that has a sign that says, 'Soulless Ink'. I've gotten three tattoos since I left my entire life behind, and maybe this is a sign that I need another.

"Yo, I'll be right with ya," a man calls from somewhere in the back when I enter.

"No rush."

"Take a look at the binders while you wait," he calls. "Get an idea of what we can do here."

It's another forty-five minutes before a woman

comes out of what I assume is the artist's tattooing space, and she's followed by a large man wearing a leather cut.

"You're still here," he says.

"I am."

"Python, I can't thank you enough," the woman gushes as he gets her checked out. "I knew you'd get it right."

"I'm just glad you trusted me with it," he tells her.

Once she's gone, Python turns his attention to me. His expression is somber, which is odd considering how fucking big and mean he looks.

"It's always the memorial tats that get me," he says. "Most people want stupid shit, but those memorials…"

It's at this moment that I know exactly what my next tattoo is going to be. "Up for another one?" I ask him.

"A tat? Always."

"A memorial one?"

"Aw, hell," he grumps. "Yeah, kid. I got you."

An hour and a half later, I inspect the new ink in the mirror. The black lines form three heartbeats, and a knife, tipped in blood, slashes through them. In bold script font, my sister's name is bright pink because that was her favorite color.

"Who's Ally?" Python asks as we walk out to the reception area. Neither of us had talked while he worked, and I'm sure he's dying to know the story.

"My sister."

"And the three heartbeats?"

Pointing my finger at each one, I reply, "Ally, my mom, and my dad."

"Damn, man."

"Yeah."

"What happened, if you don't mind me asking?"

My lungs seize, and it takes several long minutes to get any words out. "Ally's husband killed them all."

Python's eyes widen. "Fuck."

"Yeah." After paying, I step back from the counter. "Well, thanks. I need to get back on the road."

"Where ya headed?" he asks.

I shrug. "Wherever my bike takes me."

"You ride?"

"Yeah. My dad had an old Harley from when he was younger, and we rebuilt it together so I could have it on my sixteenth birthday." My heart skips a beat at the memory.

"Listen, if you really don't have a destination in mind, why don't you stick around for a while? I'm gonna be closing up soon, and there's an open party at the clubhouse tonight. Have a little fun before you take off."

"Clubhouse?"

Python turns around so I can see the back of his cut. "Soulless Kings MC. I gotta say, I think you may have stumbled into a place where your people are."

"My people?"

"Bikers, kid."

I didn't know it at the time, but Python was right. I found my people that night, along with my purpose.

CHAPTER 1
ROXIE

All I've managed to do is trade the devil I knew for the devil I'm still learning.

Present day...

"Hey, Roxanne."

I let Greg wrap his arms around me in a hug and manage to hide the wince when his touch hits the hidden bruises beneath my clothes. Jace, my fiancé, laid into me last night after accusing me of cheating when I was running late getting home from work. Moving to Boston was supposed to be a chance at a new life, but all it's gotten me is more pain and misery to last a lifetime.

"Hi," I greet him when his arms fall to his sides.

"We weren't sure you were gonna make it," Melody says, standing next to Greg.

Smiling tightly, I say, "Yeah, sorry it's been so long. Things are crazy at home."

At least that much is true. Between work and wedding planning, my time is filled with shit to do. For two years, we've always met for dinner on a weekly basis, but lately, I'm lucky to participate once a month.

"Anything we can help with?" Sammie, the fourth member of our friend group, asks.

I shake my head. "No. Jace and I have things under control."

They stare at me as if trying to mind-control the truth from my lips, but I stand firm.

"Well, all you have to do is ask," Greg finally says. "And we'll be there."

"I know, and I appreciate it."

I follow them to the table in the corner they were sitting at when I arrived. None of us needs to see the menu, as this is our usual place to dine, and as soon as we place our orders, the conversation returns to me.

"How are the wedding plans coming?" Melody asks.

I release a sigh, wanting to talk about something else, *anything* else, and realizing my friends aren't gonna let me off that easily. "Good. We've got the venue booked, and save the dates are going out next week. We meet with a few caterers tomorrow, and I've got several appointments scheduled at bridal boutiques to look for a dress. Those aren't until next month, though."

"Sounds like things are coming along," Greg says after taking a sip of his wine.

"They are."

A few minutes later, our meals are delivered, and we eat in comfortable silence. I met the three of them a week after moving to Boston. They were roommates in the apartment down the hall from mine, and we quickly became friends. Now, I don't know what I'd do without them.

"Are you going to make it next week?" Sammie asks as we walk out of the restaurant an hour later.

"Yeah," I reply. "I'll be here with bells on."

Unless Jace gets careless again.

We each go our separate ways, and when I reach my car, my phone pings from inside my purse. After sliding into the driver's seat, I pull the cell out of my purse and see a text from Jace.

> Jace: Where r u????

> Me: Just leaving the restaurant to head home

Three dots bounce on the screen as he types a

reply. They disappear several times before taunting me for a full minute, causing me to groan.

> Jace: I don't know why u insist on spending time with those people. We're getting married so u don't need them anymore. Get ur ass home. I'm hungry and tired of waiting on u.

Every cell in my body wants to tell him to fuck off, but I know that will only result in pain for me, so I don't bother. I'm tired and would like a relatively peaceful night for once.

> Me: I'll be home soon. Do you want me to pick something up for you?

> Jace: What I want is u to prepare a meal for me, but I'll settle if I have to

> Me: I'll pick up a steak dinner from your favorite place

I grind my teeth as I type the words and hit send. Jace's favorite place is thirty minutes in the opposite direction of our home, but I'd rather do that than cook for him. I call and place the order before pulling away from the curb and heading east.

Almost an hour and a half later, I pull into our

driveway and park. When I step inside, Jace is pacing the living room, and he glares at me.

"What took so long?" he snaps.

"I had to have them redo your steak," I tell him. "I ordered it medium rare, and the one they tried to give me was medium well."

His tense shoulders slump, and he quirks the corner of his mouth up. "Oh. Well, thank you."

I force a smile as I hand him the bag with his meal. "You're welcome."

"Come sit with me while I eat," he orders, turning to stalk toward the kitchen.

Rolling my eyes, I walk to the dining room and sit, waiting for him to join me. All I want to do is take a hot bath and crawl into bed, but it doesn't seem like that'll be happening any time soon.

"So," he says as he sits at the head of the table. "I've come to a decision."

"Oh?"

"I'm moving the wedding up," he announces.

My eyes widen. "But... We've already booked the venue, Jace," I remind him. "And the save the dates are already back from the printer."

He waves a hand dismissively, almost dislodging the asparagus on the end of the fork he's holding. "We won't need them. There's not enough time to send them anyway."

My stomach knots. "And the venue?"

"I've already called and rebooked it for two weeks from Saturday."

"Why the hurry?" I ask, doing my best not to vomit. "We still have so much to do."

"My assistant is taking care of everything," he says as if that makes it all better. "All you have to do is find a dress."

"Your assistant?"

His gaze snaps to mine. "Is that a problem?"

You mean other than the fact that she's made it no secret that she wants to fuck you?

"No, no problem."

If I'm being honest with myself, I couldn't care less if he bangs her. The more he takes his aggression out on someone else, the less I have to hurt.

Fuck, that makes me sound like a cold-hearted bitch.

"Anyway, you'll pick out a dress tomorrow and bring it by the office so I can give my stamp of approval."

"I..." I swallow past the lump in my throat. "Okay."

He eats the rest of his dinner in silence, leaving me to stew about how I've lost myself in the darkness that is him.

I ran from my hometown to escape alpha assholes

and the misogynistic lifestyle of my brother's club, Limitless Throttle MC, but all I've managed to do is trade the devil I knew for the devil I'm still learning.

CHAPTER 2
SCREAMER

I never thought I'd want something like that.

"What are you still doing here?"

I glance over my shoulder at Jared, my boss at the bike shop, and smirk. We closed hours ago, but the owner of the Harley Fatboy I'm working on wants his bike back by the end of the week, so I stayed behind to get caught up.

"Wouldn't have to be here so late if you'd hire more people," I quip.

Jared chuckles. We've had this argument numerous times, and Journey, my VP, and I are determined to convince him that it's not only a good idea but necessary as fuck.

"Quality over quantity," he says, using the same old argument.

Grabbing the rag from the floor next to me, I wipe the grease from my hands as I stand to face him. "We're already sacrificing quality with the way we're taking on projects. It's time to bite the bullet, boss man."

Jared walks around the motorcycle, admiring my work, and finally stops to stand next to me. "Fine. I'll start putting feelers out. Unless you've got someone in mind?"

I arch a brow. "Seriously? You're actually going to hire someone?"

He shrugs. "I know you and Journey think I don't listen, but I do. And you're right... We need more mechanics. Shit, we need someone else who can do custom projects, as well." Pausing, he runs his hand over his long gray beard. "Besides, the wife's getting on me about retiring soon. Guess now is as good a time as any to beef up the place."

My mind buzzes at this new piece of information. Jared opened the shop almost thirty years ago, and he's busted his ass to make it the legend it is among bikers. I thought for sure he'd work until he had both feet in the grave.

I whistle. "You gonna sell or..."

He grins. "Why? You looking to buy?"

Fuck, yes.

"I mean, I think the club would be interested for sure," I say nonchalantly.

Soulless Kings MC owns Sinful Wheels up in Oregon, and I know Fender and Crow have talked about opening a location here in Marble Falls, but they also know that there's no way a new shop could compete with what Jared's built.

My boss is quiet for a minute before saying, "Get me a sit-down with Crow, and we can go from there."

I nod. "I can do that."

"Are you serious?"

I lift my beer and grin at Journey. As soon as I arrived at the clubhouse, I filled him in on my conversation with Jared, and his eyes lit up.

"As serious as having to lay your bike down," I say.

"Yo, Crow!" he hollers, and our president turns in his chair from across the room. "C'mere, brother."

Crow wraps his arms around his old lady, Addison, and shakes his head. "Whatever it is, it can wait." He turns away from us, effectively shutting down any more conversation.

Journey rolls his eyes. "Pussy-whipped bastard," he mutters.

I slap Journey on the back. "You're one to talk," I remind him. "If Wren were here, you'd be all over her, and the shop would be the last thing on your mind."

He shrugs. "True."

"When's she due home?" I ask, knowing he hates being away from his old lady.

He pulls his cell from his cut and looks at the time. "Any minute, actually," he says as he rises from his stool.

I watch him walk away, jealousy slithering through me like a snake. Shoving the unwelcome feeling from my mind, I spin on my stool and rest my forearms on the bar. Lately, it seems like all my brothers are getting hitched, and I never thought I'd want something like that.

My mind swirls with memories, reminders of why I despise relationships. My parents had a great relationship, but in the end, their love couldn't save them. And my sister? Fuck, if ever I needed a reason to refuse to get tied down, it's her marriage.

But I'd be lying if I didn't admit that my brothers have found something that, at least on the surface, is enviable.

"Why so serious?"

I slide my eyes to the right and see Sunny, a club whore, staring at me. Her bright red lips are curved into a smile, and her eyes are a dull green. She's been *serving* Soulless Kings MC for a few years now, and it shows.

"No reason," I reply with a shrug before draining the rest of my beer.

Sunny reaches toward me and drags a long, pointy fingernail down my covered chest. "Keep telling yourself that, baby." She licks her lips. "How 'bout we go to your room, and I'll help you forget all about what's troubling you?"

Sunny isn't my favorite club whore, but I'm not stupid. Fucking is the one thing guaranteed to override my memories, even if it is temporary.

"You think you can handle me?" I ask, knowing that if I take her to my room, I'm going to be rough, demanding, and on a mission to forget.

"Bring it on, baby."

CHAPTER 3
ROXIE

I TRIED SO HARD TO PUT IT ALL BEHIND ME.

"HAVE A GOOD NIGHT."

Shutting the door behind our guests, I lock it before turning around. I don't have time to brace myself for the slap Jace delivers. My cheek stings, and tears well in my eyes.

"What the hell?" I mutter.

"The next time we have people over for dinner, try not to flirt with anyone who has a penis," he snarls as he reaches out to grab a fistful of my hair.

Jace drags me from the entryway and shoves me to the floor in the living room. He came home from work in a snit, and I was hoping that time with friends would improve his mood, but apparently it didn't.

"I wasn't flirting," I insist, just as his foot connects with my ribs.

Jace wasn't like this before we got engaged, but it's like the moment he had a ring on my finger, a switch flipped. He became possessive, jealous, controlling, and, more recently, physical.

Shame washes over me as I curl into a ball to ward off more kicks.

If my brother could see me now...

Shuffle is the president of the one percent motorcycle club, Limitless Throttle MC, and he'd be disgusted if he saw his little sister not standing up for herself. He, along with the other brothers in the MC, taught me better than this. So much fucking better.

But you ran from them, from that life.

"Then what the fuck was that shit with Bradley?" he snarls. "You were all over him."

I search my brain for what he's talking about, and the only thing that comes to mind is when my hand brushed Bradley's when I handed him the bottle of wine so he could top his glass off.

"Jesus, that's what this is about?" I ask, knowing I should just keep my mouth shut.

He stiffens above me. "What the hell else would it be about? Oh, wait..." Jace leans down and yanks on the strap of my dress. "Maybe this slutty scrap of cloth."

The strap snaps, and he pulls the material down my body until I'm in nothing but the black thong and kitten heels I'm wearing. Jace bought me the outfit a few weeks ago when we planned tonight's dinner, so I don't know what his problem is with it now.

I try to cross my arms over my bare chest, but he kicks my arms to stop the movement. Bending to grab a fistful of my hair, he drags me across the room toward the stairs.

"Get up," he demands after releasing me. I scramble to my feet, and he shoves me forward. "Fucking walk."

"I'm trying," I snap as I take the first step, then the next.

Unsatisfied with my speed, Jace pushes past me and grabs my arm to pull me up the steps behind him. "I don't have time for your shit," he snarls.

"What shit?" I ask.

He doesn't respond as he takes me into the bedroom. "Don't move," he orders before dropping my arm and storming into the adjoining bath.

My mind spins as I recall the events of the evening. I can't pinpoint the exact moment Jace's anger took over. Lately, it's become increasingly difficult to dissect his moods and spot red flags. While I wait for him to return from the bathroom, one thought keeps popping into my mind: What more can he do to me?

Murder.

That word enters my brain unbidden, and I cringe at how easily it came. I've been around violence, death, and all sorts of bad shit, but I tried so hard to put it all behind me.

"I told you not to move," Jace barks when he steps back into the bedroom.

I snap my head up at his voice and realize that, at some point, I sat on the edge of the bed. He stalks toward me, rage turning his cheeks a deep red, and slams his fist into my face when he reaches me.

Time passes in a blur as he continues to deliver blow after blow. I do my best to fight back, but it's useless. I've never experienced Jace's wrath when he's this far gone, and I'm unable to anticipate his moves because his actions are all over the place.

By the time he stomps out of the room, my entire body is on fire, and I can barely move. Blood is spattered all over the comforter, floor, and walls. Agony tears through me as I try to get to my feet.

I collapse three times before I make it to the door. Bracing myself against the frame, I try to catch my breath, but inhaling threatens to send me to my knees. I take a moment to mentally catalogue my injuries.

Broken ribs… check.

Unknown number of bruises… check.

Possible broken cheekbone… check.

Beyond that, I have no idea. And honestly, I'm not sure I want to know. Tears stream down my cheeks, and the salty taste mixes with the blood when they reach my lips. I lift my arm, ignoring the pain, and brush away the wetness.

I'm exhausted, but I can't stop. I need to get to my cell downstairs. When Jace was done, I heard the front door slam, so I know he's gone, but I have no clue how much time I have before he returns.

When I finally make it to the first floor, every inch of me wants to fall onto the couch and pass out, but I force myself to go to the kitchen and grab my phone off the counter.

> Me: I need u guys… 911

I hit send and the message appears in the group thread I have with Sammie, Greg, and Melody. For all I know, they could be busy, but I'm counting on at least one of them seeing the text and coming to my rescue.

Almost instantly, my phone pings multiple times with responses.

> Greg: What happened?

> Melody: On my way

> Greg: Be there in 10

> Sammie: Gotta throw on clothes but I'm coming

> Melody: Need police?

> Sammie: Ambulance?

>> Me: No police or ambo. Jace lost his shit. Gotta get outta here

> Greg: I'll kill him!

> Sammie: Bringing the shovel!

> Melody: I have no prob digging a grave

Relief floods my system at their reaction. I collapse on the couch and wait for them to arrive. As I wait, my brain races. I need to leave, get as far away from Jace as I can, but I'm pretty sure driving right now is out of the question.

What other choice do you have?

I may have lost my way and become his doormat, but I refuse to let it continue. He took it too far tonight, and I'll be damned if I do nothing.

"Rox, where are you?"

Sammie's voice pulls me from my thoughts, and I

try to sit up. "On the couch," I call out when I can't stand.

She rushes around the sofa until she stands in front of me.

"Motherfucker," she breaths. "You're leaving him, Rox. I don't care how much you love him, but there's no excuse for this."

I nod. "I know."

"I'm here!" Greg calls out from the entryway.

"We're in the living room," Sammie replies. "And brace yourself because it's not pretty."

I wince at her words, knowing I have to look terrible. Shit, I feel terrible.

"Oh my God," Greg mutters when he sees me. "Jace did this?"

"Of course, Jace did this," Sammie snaps.

"What did Jace…" Melody's voice trails off when she joins the other two in front of me. "That's it, you're leaving… tonight."

"I know," I repeat. "But I don't think I can drive."

My three friends exchange a look, but it's Sammie who offers an alternative. "I'll drive you a few hours away and get you settled into a hotel. You could come to one of our houses, but he'd find you there."

"I can't ask you—"

"You're not asking," Melody snaps.

I release a breath and nod. "Yeah, okay."

"My SUV can fit quite a bit, so let's get everything we can and load it up," Sammie states. "You're not coming back for anything."

More tears fill my eyes. "I... I don't think... I don't think I can help pack anything," I admit.

"That's fine," Greg says with a sympathetic smile. "Just tell us what to get, and we'll do the rest."

Melody lifts her hand like she's a student in class. "Uh, any clue when Jace'll be back?" I shake my head. "Then let's make this quick."

Thirty minutes later, Greg is helping me into the passenger seat of Sammie's vehicle, and the back is loaded down with my things. Once I'm settled, he kisses me on the cheek.

"I'm gonna miss you," he tells me. "But as long as you're safe, that's all that matters."

My throat clogs with emotion. The pain is now bearable thanks to the pain pill Melody gave me. Fortunately, she had a tooth pulled earlier in the week and had one to spare. She put the rest of her prescription in my purse despite my protests, insisting that I needed it more than she did.

"I can't thank you enough," I say to Greg and Melody, who's now standing next to him.

"I hate to break this up, but we should go," Sammie says as she slides into the driver's seat and starts the engine.

"Right," Melody states. "Maybe this would be a good time for you to reconnect with your family."

"Maybe," I whisper, knowing the last place I can go is to my brother. At least, not until I've healed.

"Be safe," Greg says as he closes the door.

"Ready?" Sammie asks, putting the SUV in gear.

I swallow past the lump in my throat. "As I'll ever be."

CHAPTER 4
SCREAMER

LIFE IS GOOD.

"Gotta say, I'm surprised you're retiring."

Jarod smirks at Crow as Journey and I sit back. Crow wanted to meet with Jarod as soon as I told him the club had a chance of buying his shop, but I was surprised when Jarod agreed to meet. I thought for sure he'd back out.

"The missus says it's time," Jarod says with a shrug. "She wants to spend more time with the grandkids and travel, and I can't deny her that. She's put up with way too much over the years from me."

Crow chuckles. "So that's what I have to look forward to with Addi… nagging to get me to do less with the club?"

"Happy wife, happy life," my boss jokes.

"Maybe I'll get lucky," Journey chimes in. "With Wren's different personalities, one of 'em's bound to be okay with me riding till I die."

Jarod throws his head back and laughs. "Good luck with that."

"If Peg has anything to say about it," I begin, referring to the personality that doles out punishment. "You'll be outta the club by the time you're forty."

Journey groans. It took him a while to sort through the different identities Wren has, but he's managed. In fact, we don't see a lot of them anymore because Wren's therapist has really been helping.

"Let's get down to business," Crow states, refocusing the conversation. "Do you have a price in mind for the shop?"

Jarod arches a brow. "Do you?"

My pres grins. "Of course," he says before giving a number.

"Wow, that's generous," Jarod says.

"It's fair," Journey comments. "We've all discussed what the club can afford, as well as what we think the shop is worth. It's understood that it took you years and a lot of blood, sweat, and tears to get the shop where it is today. You've built a solid reputation in the community, and we recognize that you deserve to be compensated for more than just the building."

We spend the next hour going over details of the sale, and by the time Jarod leaves, the Soulless Kings MC owns another business. There are stipulations to the sale, such as we cannot turn away any current customers, and Jarod wants to stay on part-time. The sale won't be final for another three months, which gives him time to adjust, and plenty of time to find some new employees and get them trained.

"Can you believe it?" Journey asks after Jarod leaves.

"Fuck, no," I say with a chuckle. "I thought we were getting our hopes up for nothing. That man lives and breathes the shop."

Crow slaps me on the back. "It might seem like it, but he lives for his family. You'd understand that if you ever settled down."

I shake my head. "Nope, not happening." Walking toward the door, I add, "I'm outta here."

My brothers' laughter follows me down the hallway. They know my stance on relationships and why I have an aversion to them, but it doesn't seem to stop them from throwing out jabs every now and then, especially now that they're all tied down to a woman.

"Is it done?" Stunner, our treasurer, asks when I enter the main room.

"It is," I say with a grin. "There'll be a Sinful Wheels in Marble Falls in three months."

"You gonna talk to Jimmy about working there?" he asks, referring to one of the prospects.

"Yeah, I will," I confirm. "Kid's a killer mechanic, and he knows his shit when it comes to custom projects."

"I know he'll be thrilled," Stunner says. "Whenever he's here, all he does is talk about bikes."

It's true. Jimmy is a gearhead, and now that Journey and I will be in charge of hiring, we can bring him on board.

After talking with Stunner for a few more minutes, I head outside to go into the shop. As always, when I'm on my Harley, I feel alive, unburdened, happy. But when I arrive at the shop and see a familiar motorcycle, my stomach drops.

"'Bout time you got here," Shuffle states as I enter through the front.

The president of Limitless Throttle MC isn't an enemy. In fact, I consider him a friend, but he never shows up without an appointment unless he has information I'm not gonna like.

"What're you doing here?" I ask.

He shrugs. "Was in the neighborhood, and a little

birdie told me that the shop'll be transitioning to new owners. Just came to congratulate you."

"Jesus, word travels fast," I mutter.

Shuffle laughs. "Nah. Crow called to fill me in since Limitless Throttle owns the laundry mat down the road. He wanted to make sure I knew y'all weren't encroaching on our territory."

"No interest in anything here other than this shop," I tell him. "You'll have no trouble from us."

"Fuck, I know that," he says.

"Good. Now, can I get to work?" I snap, itching to get through some of the repairs waiting for me in the back.

Shuffle taps the counter. "Sure thing. Why don't you come down and see me when you're done here tonight? We can go grab a drink to celebrate."

"I can do that."

"Good. See ya later."

"Later."

After he leaves, I get to work. The day passes in a blur, but I can't remember the last time I felt this content at the shop. Things are falling into place in a way I thought wouldn't happen, and life is good.

CHAPTER 5
ROXIE

I need to feel safe.

"Where are you?"

I roll my eyes at the concern in my brother's voice. It's been two weeks since I left Jace, and I've slowly been making my way to Marble Falls. I checked into my current hotel two nights ago, and once I check out, I'll finish the trip. I haven't talked to Shuffle in roughly a month, but when he called this morning, the urge to talk to him was strong.

"Well, that's the thing. I'm—"

"And why is Jace calling me, asking if I've seen you?" he demands without giving me a chance to answer his first question.

Groaning, I put the call on speaker and toss it

onto the bed before flopping onto my back. "Are you gonna let me talk?" I counter.

My brother sighs. "Yeah, fine."

"I'm a few hours from you," I admit before swallowing past the lump in my throat. "I, um, am moving back."

The bruises have faded and can be completely covered with makeup, and the pain from my other injuries is bearable. The last thing I wanted to do was return to the control of my brother and the club, but it's also the only place I know I'll be safe.

And I need to feel safe.

I've spoken to Sammie, Greg, and Melody, and they've been keeping an eye on Jace as best they can. They've each assured me that he seems to be going about life like nothing happened, but that's little comfort now that I know he's called Shuffle.

"Rox, what the fuck is going on?" he demands, pulling me back to the conversation.

Taking a deep breath, I decide to lie my ass off. "Jace broke off the engagement, and it was too hard to be in the same town as him. I figured you'd be happy about me coming back."

"I *am* happy," he insists. "But you were so fucking hell bent to leave me and everything else behind, and I find it hard to believe that something as trivial as a break-up is what's changed your mind."

"Jesus," I mutter. "Maybe I should just go somewhere else."

"Dammit, Rox, stop," Shuffle barks.

"No, Ryan," I snap, using his given name. "I won't stop. I left for a reason, and coming back isn't easy."

Silence fills the room, and when I lift the phone to see if he disconnected the call, he sighs. "When will you be here?"

"Within the next few days," I reply begrudgingly because there's no point in continuing to argue.

"How long are you staying?"

"How's Titan?" I ask, ignoring his question since I don't have an answer. I'll stay as long as I need to, and I'm hoping that's not long.

He chuckles. "Miss your bike, huh?"

I practically groan. "You have no idea," I admit.

"I still don't know why you didn't take it with you when you left."

"Because… I couldn't exactly fit all my shit on a Harley."

"Okay, but why didn't you ever come back for it or have me ship it to you?"

Because my asshole fiancé wasn't exactly the type to be okay with his significant other riding a motorcycle.

"Never mind," he says when I remain silent. "So, I'll see ya in a few days?"

"Yep."

My brother inhales deeply, and in that breath, I hear his worry. "You sure you don't want me to send someone to come get you?"

I smile sadly, glad that he can't see me. "I'm sure, Ry. I'm fine, I promise. Just want a few more days to clear my head." *And to heal a bit more.*

"Okay, then I'll see you soon."

The sound of shuffling comes through the line, and I know he's about to end the call.

"Hey, Ry," I say, regaining his attention.

"Yeah?"

"Love you."

"Right back at ya, kid."

CHAPTER 6
SCREAMER

MEMORIES EQUAL PAIN.

"Is this really necessary?"

I glance in the rearview mirror at the man trussed up in the back of the utility van. Ghost, Poker, and I were tasked with picking him up and bringing him to the clubhouse for interrogation in the Nightmare Room, and that's exactly what we're doing. But if he doesn't shut the fuck up, he's not going to make it to the Nightmare Room. Shit, he won't make it to our exit if he keeps whining.

"Carter, my man," Ghost begins. "You brought this on yourself. Maybe you shoulda taken your vows a bit more seriously."

Carter Mathis is a thirty-year-old prick who chose to step out on his wife. Cheating spouses isn't something the Soulless Kings MC gets involved in, but unfortunately for him, he also has a penchant for using his fists when he doesn't get his way. Bastard's wife is Molly's cousin, and Molly is a club whore.

When Molly's cousin, Janice, showed up at the clubhouse with bruises covering her face and neck, the club was asked to intervene. Even club whores are considered family, which puts them and their loved ones under our protection.

"What does Janice have to do with this?" Carter demands, struggling against his restraints.

"Aw, that's cute," Poker states comically. "He really doesn't have a fucking clue."

"Whatever that bitch is sa—"

The van shakes from the force of Ghost's punch, and Carter's words turn into cries of pain. "That *bitch* is your wife," Ghost seethes.

Before Carter can say anything else, Poker grabs a roll of Duct tape and covers his mouth. I want to demand that he take it off so I can listen to this fuck's pathetic excuses and pleas for his life, but I know the smart thing to do is hold in my rage until we're back at the clubhouse.

An hour and a half later, my brothers and I are carrying the man around to the back entrance that leads straight downstairs to the Nightmare Room. I'd prefer to drag him, but his struggles made that impossible.

As soon as the large door slides closed behind us, we drop Carter to the concrete floor, and he does his best to scramble into the corner.

"Now he's scared," Ghost grumbles.

I stalk toward the cowering prick and yank the tape from his mouth, grinning when I see blood where the skin was ripped off. Crumbling the tape, I throw it to the floor.

"Grab me the torch," I demand and hear my brothers snicker behind me. Five seconds later, the device is handed to me over my shoulder. I keep my eyes locked on Carter's as I turn the knob, and blue flame shoots from the nozzle. "This might hurt," I taunt.

His screams fill the room as I burn him alive, and my mind transposes another man's face over his.

Twenty-one years old...

"Are you sure about this?"

I swallow my fear and nod. When I started prospecting with Soulless Kings MC, I had no fucking clue how my life would change. It's been three years since my family died and a year and a half since their murderer was deemed incompetent to stand trial and admitted to the state hospital for treatment.

"I need the words, Screamer," Crow snaps. "Because if you aren't, we need to get the fuck outta here."

I stare at the rundown brick building across the street, the one with equally rundown barbed wire fencing surrounding it. "I'm sure. Brian has to pay for what he did."

Journey slaps me on the back. "Then let's do this."

After I was made a fully patched member of the club, I went to Crow and Journey and told them about my plans to make Brian pay for killing my sister and parents. They knew the story, knew what had me running from my past, and they agreed to help me.

It took a while to plan, but now that I'm here, minutes away from kidnapping the sick fuck from a facility that should be impenetrable, I'm scared. Don't get me wrong, I'm not afraid of getting caught or even of what the guy could do to me if he manages to get the upper hand. No, I'm fucking terrified because looking at him, being face to face with him… it makes me think of Ally. It forces me to remember, and I hate remembering.

Memories equal pain.

Twenty minutes later, Crow, Journey, and I are back in the van with the man of the hour. Brian didn't put up a fight when I entered his room—courtesy of my Pres and VP's distraction—, and he isn't resisting now. He's sitting in the back of the cargo van like a choir boy waiting for his solo to begin.

What the hell?

"I thought you said he was crazy," Journey states, glancing in the rearview mirror at me as he drives. "Seems pretty tame to me."

"I said he convinced everyone else that he's crazy," I bark. "He's as sane as they come with a heavy dose of evil sprinkled in."

"My favorite," Crow says, rubbing his hands together. He turns in the passenger seat to glare at Brian. "You should've gone to trial. Jail woulda been easier than what my man, Screamer, has planned for you."

Brian scoffs, and it's the first sound he's made since he calmly said 'hello' to me earlier. "Ben doesn't scare me."

My blood boils, and my body heats with rage. "It's Screamer," I snarl. "You killed Ben, same as you did his whole goddamn family."

He has the audacity to tilt his head and smile. "You're proving my point. You're nothing but a weak waste of space who can't do anything for himself. You always needed your sister to fight your battles for you, and now you've got them." He nods at Crow and Journey. "Pathetic."

I clench my fists to keep from ending him right here, right now. The Nightmare Room awaits me, and that's where I'll get my revenge. Normally, as the Road Captain, I'm not the one to inflict punishment, but Crow promised me that I could do whatever the fuck I want to Brian.

I want to kill him.

Journey chuckles at Brian's statement. "Damn, man, you're in for the surprise of your life."

"We'll see," Brian says before leaning back against the side of the van like he doesn't have a care in the world.

"Yeah," I agree. "We will."

CHAPTER 7
ROXIE

I JUST WANT A PLACE TO LICK MY WOUNDS.

STARING AT THE PLACE THAT I USED TO CALL HOME, I take a deep breath and remind myself that being here is temporary. As I open the door and get out of the car, a noise catches my attention. I whip my gaze toward the entrance to the clubhouse and see my brother standing there.

Deep breath… in, out, in, out.

"I was wondering when you were gonna get here," Shuffle says as he walks toward me. "Glad you made it safely."

He wraps his arms around me in a hug, and I find myself burning my head against his chest. I may have walked away from this place, this life, but I love my brother. For the first time since I left Jace, I feel... safe.

Sniffling back tears, I pull away and turn to grab one of my bags from the back seat. "Help me with my stuff?"

He moves to stand next to me and glance into the vehicle. "Yo, boys, get your lazy asses out here," he shouts to the club brothers who are no doubt standing just inside the door waiting for me.

One by one, they file outside. I recognize each man, and my knees threaten to buckle at the happiness I see when they look at me.

"Welcome home, Rox," Bear says, lifting me off my feet when he reaches me.

"Put me down," I grumble even as my arms go around his neck.

I need this. I need to feel safe with people I know and trust.

As soon as he releases me, I'm swept into another set of arms. "Damn, girl, you're a sight for sore eyes," Chains comments just before he passes me to another brother.

"Glad you finally came to your fuckin' senses," Blush teases after kissing my cheek.

"Stop," I snap before Creep can get his hands on me, and he freezes, a shocked expression on his face.

"Sorry. It's just..." I blow out a breath. "I'm fucking tired, guys. Can't this little love fest wait until I get inside at least?"

Shuffle narrows his eyes on me for a moment, but then he reminds me why I love him so much. "You heard her. All of you, grab some of her shit and take it to her room. You can welcome her home later."

Each of them mumbles but do as they're told. When it's just me and my brother, I soften my expression and give him a grateful smile.

"Thanks."

"Don't thank me," he gripes. "Just because you're getting a reprieve now doesn't mean I'm not going to grill your ass later."

With that, he turns on his heel and carries two duffels into the clubhouse, leaving me to follow. After grabbing the last box that remains in the car, I lock the doors and stride inside.

Shuffle is waiting for me across the room, and I walk toward him, forcing a smile for anyone who says 'hello'. When I'm a few feet away, he closes the distance between us and wraps an arm around my shoulder.

"C'mon," he says, calmer than he was outside.

We move down the hallway, stopping when we reach the door to my room, the same room I had before I left years ago. I open the door, and my breath catches in my throat.

"It's..." I lift my eyes to his. "You kept it the same?"

He shrugs. "Of course, I did. This is your home, Rox."

Entering the room, I drop the box I'm carrying on the floor. Shuffle does the same with the bags in his hand, and I jump at the noise. Quickly masking the reaction, I face him.

"I think I'm gonna take a shower," I say, desperate to be alone.

He jerks a nod. "Yeah, okay."

My brother turns to walk away, but I stop him. "Hey, um..." He glances over his shoulder at me. "Where's my bike?"

Shuffle grins, and for the first time since he hugged me, it reaches his eyes. "It's in the garage behind the clubhouse."

"Ridable?"

"Yeah."

Relief floods my system. I wasn't lying when I told him I was going to shower, but as soon as I'm done, I'm riding. I *need* to ride.

"Great." I twist my hands. "Thanks."

"Want me to ride with you?" he asks, his tone hopeful.

"Nah." I shake my head. "I think I just want to be alone."

Pointing a finger at me, his expression instantly hardens. "That shit's gotta stop," he snaps. "You're not alone, Rox. Never have been and never will be."

"I didn't mean it like that," I insist.

"Bullshit."

"Ryan, please." I rub my temples to stave off the forming migraine. "I don't want to fight with you. I just… Give me some time to settle in before—"

"Before what?" he snaps. "Before I demand the truth? Before I call you out on every single lie you've told me the last few days? What the fuck do you want from me, Rox?"

Staring at the floor, I let a tear fall from my eye. "I want…" I lift my head and level my gaze at him. "I just want a place to lick my wounds."

His eyes narrow. "Fine. Lick 'em. But if you leave after, don't think you'll be able to roll up in here again like nothing happened."

With that, he storms out of my room, yanking the door shut behind him. His retreating footsteps filter through the barrier, but it's only seconds before I hear them thudding back to my room.

"Rox, your bike is good to ride, but it should be looked over before you go too far," he says, his voice low. "You're fine today, but when you're ready, I'll take you to the shop in town, and we'll get it serviced, okay?"

I know he won't leave until I respond, so I say, "Okay." Again, his footsteps thud in retreat. "Thanks, Ryan," I whisper to myself before heading to the shower.

CHAPTER 8
SCREAMER

I GET THE FEELING THAT BEING TUNED INTO THINGS ABOUT THIS PARTICULAR WOMAN IS GOING TO CAUSE ME A WORLD OF TROUBLE.

"Have a good one."

Another satisfied customer walks out of the shop, and I sag onto the stool behind the counter. When I'm not neck deep in club business, I'm here working on bikes. I'm fucking exhausted, and I don't see a light at the end of this particular tunnel. Not that I mind. Exhaustion is better than keyed up from memories and nightmares.

The door between the front and back of the shop swings open, and Journey steps through. "What the hell are you doing?"

I scrub my hands over my face and sigh. "Nothing."

"Exactly," he says, hitching a thumb over his shoulder. "There's work to be done."

I rise to my feet and glare at him. "Don't you thin—"

The jingle of the bell above the entrance forces me to shut my mouth and turn to face the newcomer. When I see Shuffle walk inside, I roll my eyes. He throws his head back and laughs at me.

"Is that any way to greet a customer?" he asks.

"Customer my ass," I gripe, no heat in my words. "What can I do for ya?"

Shuffle looks over his shoulder, and I follow his gaze through the large window and freeze when my eyes land on a beautiful woman getting off a Harley at the curb. I try to form words, but nothing comes out.

"Didn't know you had a girlfriend," Journey says, breaking the silence just as the woman steps inside behind Shuffle.

"Fucking hell," she mutters, stepping around the man.

Her eyes widen when they land on me and Journey, and if I were a bettin' man, I'd wager my custom bike that it's fear causing the look. She shifts closer to the biker.

Shuffle shakes his head. "This is Roxie, my sister." He points at us. "Rox, this is Screamer and Journey.

They're Soulless Kings, but they're damn good with bikes, so I overlook that," he jokes.

Roxie glances around the front of the shop, her eyes taking in everything but Journey and me. All of a sudden, her smart mouth seems incapable of speech.

"Nice to meet you," I say, stepping up to the counter and leaning on it.

"Rox needs to have her Harley serviced," Shuffle states. "Can you squeeze her in?"

I could squeeze her in all right. Or would it be me squeezing into her?

I shake the thought from my head and do my best to ignore the boner in my pants. Even in the ripped jeans and tattered hoodie, Roxie is stunning. Large blue eyes, a pert nose, pouty lips, and hips that beg to be straddled make up the vision I know is going into my spank bank.

Yeah, fine, I'm an asshole.

Journey moves to stand next to me and pulls up the schedule on the computer. He peers at the screen for several seconds before looking at Shuffle. "We're pretty booked, but we have an ope—"

"I can work on the bike after hours," I blurt, and Journey's gaze whips to mine. I shrug off his scrutiny. "What? Limitless Throttle brings a lot of business our way. It's the least I can do for a loyal customer."

"I knew I liked you for a reason," Shuffle says.

"You like me because I'm the only mechanic crazy enough to deal with your ass," I retort.

"I, um…" Roxie speaks, but her eyes are on the floor. "I don't want to put you out."

"If he says he can do it, Rox, he can do it," her brother tells her. "Don't worry 'bout it."

"Why don't I get your information, and I can get you into the computer?" Journey suggests.

"Yeah, okay."

Journey asks her questions for the next several minutes. Shuffle moves to sit in one of the chairs along the wall, and I stand here like an idiot.

"That should do it," Journey finally says. "If you leave the bike, Screamer will get it done within the next few days."

Roxie's eyes dart from Journey to me, and there's no mistaking the apprehension there. She seemed at ease talking to my VP, so why am I eliciting this reaction?

"Got your key fob?" I ask.

Rather than answer, she nods before rushing outside. I watch as she stands next to her bike, her shoulders rising and falling as if she's taking deep breaths. After a few minutes, she reaches into her pocket and pulls something out. I squint and see that it's the key fob.

Why go outside to get it when she had it on her?

When she returns inside, she hands me the fob, and I smile. "Thanks."

Again, she just nods.

Something is going on with her, and for some reason, I am desperate to find out what that something is. Shuffle seems oblivious, but I'm not.

I don't like being oblivious, especially to women, but I get the feeling that being tuned into things about this particular woman is going to cause me a world of trouble.

CHAPTER 9
ROXIE

Stay the fuck away from Screamer.

What the fuck is wrong with me?

When Shuffle insisted that I come with him to talk to the mechanic, I hadn't put up too much of a fight because I thought it'd be Jared we were meeting. What harm could seeing an old man do? But when we arrived at the shop, Jared was nowhere to be seen, and two bikers were in his place at the counter.

Since returning home, I've been fine around men. Hell, I was when I was traveling, but the moment my eyes landed on Screamer, fear ricocheted through me like a malfunctioning pinball machine.

What's that about?

"Seriously?"

My brother's tense voice caught my attention,

and I turned to see him walk out of the shop to stand on the sidewalk.

"So, how come this is the first time we're meeting you?"

I whirl toward Journey, wincing at the jolt of pain that remains in my ribs and wondering about my lack of fear of him. "I've been gone for a few years," I admit as I move to sit in the chair my brother vacated.

"Gone?" Screamer asks, and my muscles tense at his voice.

Trying to inhale deeply, I square my shoulders. "Yeah, gone," I snap.

He holds his hands up. "Sorry. Didn't mean to touch a nerve."

It's on the tip of my tongue to make my own apology, but I refrain. The guy's done nothing wrong, yet he makes me uneasy. An awkward silence fills the space, and I find myself wishing I could disappear.

Several minutes pass, and I startle when the door bangs open, further aggravating my still healing injuries.

Maybe riding my Harley hasn't been the best idea.

My brother's expression is murderous as he faces me.

"I've gotta go," he grits. "Can you get back to the clubhouse?"

"I'll make sure she gets home," Screamer says casually, and Shuffle nods before leaving me alone with two men I don't know.

Without thinking, I jump to my feet and chase after my brother, but he's already pulling away from the curb.

"Fuck," I mutter, beginning to pace while hugging myself.

"Aw, c'mon, I'm not that bad."

I whirl around to see Screamer propping the door open with his shoulder, arms crossed over his broad chest and a grin spread across his face.

"I…" I clear my throat. "Be that as it may, I don't know you."

"Your brother trusts me."

I scoff. "That's not saying much." Sticking out my hand, I add, "I need my fob back."

He stares at me, his eyes boring into mine, and my stomach clenches at his scrutiny. The man is gorgeous and no doubt a danger to women's panties everywhere, but I'm not in the market for anything he might have to offer.

"It's really no big deal, Roxie," he says. "Gimme a few minutes to wrap things up here, and I'll drive you home."

I shift my gaze from him to the door and back

again, feeling trapped. Taking a step back and to the right, I snap, "I can get myself home."

Screamer narrows his eyes. "I'm sure you can. But don't you want me to work on your bike?"

"Maybe another time," I say and lunge past him to go inside.

"Wait a minute," he says, grabbing my arm and bringing me to a painful halt.

"Ouch," I hiss through gritted teeth, and it takes everything in me not to double over and hold my ribs. I yank free of his hold. "Don't fucking touch me."

He releases me, and I storm through the door. Journey lifts his head, his focus shifting from whatever he was doing to me.

"Forget something?" he asks, oblivious to the tension between his friend and me.

"I need my key fob," I bark.

When his eyes move to look beyond me, I glance over my shoulder in time to see Screamer shrug. Then Journey turns and grabs my fob off a hook on the wall behind him and hands it to me.

"There ya go," he says.

I sigh with relief. "Thanks."

"No problem. Whenever you're ready for us to take a look at it, just drop it off. No need to make an appointment."

I smile appreciatively, somehow at ease with him in a way I'm not with Screamer. Maybe it's the wedding band on his finger, or maybe it's the fact that I'm not attracted to him in the least.

The whys don't matter.

"I will," I lie, vowing never to return to the shop. I'll find another mechanic.

I turn on my heel and skirt past Screamer. Just before the door closes behind me, his voice reaches my ears.

"Drive safe, Roxie."

Tears fill my eyes at his words. Other than my brother and my friends, when I left Jace, no one has cared enough to say that to me in a long, damn time. You'd think a fiancé would, but looking back, Jace only ever cared about himself. If the beating I took is any indication, he certainly didn't give a fuck about me.

Rather than return to the clubhouse, I head out of town and hit the country roads. I need to get my head on straight, or I'll never survive Shuffle and the Limitless Throttle brothers.

While I ride, my mind races with the events of the last few years. I never thought I'd return to Marble Falls, but it was my only option. Sure, I technically could've gone anywhere, yet here I am. I hadn't given it a second thought when I loaded my shit into the rental car and hugged Sammie for what is likely the last time.

The two weeks I gave myself to heal should've been sufficient, but my reaction to Screamer proves how wrong I was. Maybe I should hightail it out of Texas and never look back.

Like that would help.

No, I'm not running. The solution to my problem is a very simple one…

Stay the fuck away from Screamer.

CHAPTER 10
SCREAMER

Who hurt her, and where the fuck can I find him?

"What the hell did you say to her?"

I bristle at the accusation in Journey's tone. Why is he immediately assuming I did something wrong?

"Nothing," I insist, replaying our interaction in my head. From the instant I laid eyes on Roxie, I recognized the one emotion that enrages me when a woman displays it: fear. There was also no mistaking the pain she was experiencing, despite her efforts to mask it. "Think Shuffle knows?"

Journey's forehead wrinkles in confusion. "Knows what?"

"That his sister's been knocked around," I say bluntly.

His eyes widen. "Really? You think so?"

"Bro, she was scared as fuck," I say.

He chuckles. "Of you, maybe, but what chick wouldn't be? You're intimidating, Screamer."

"So are you," I retort. "But she was fine with you."

He shrugs. "I don't know, man. She seemed more mad than scared to me."

"You seriously didn't notice the way she winced when she was slightly jostled or the way she was holding her ribs? I'm telling you, she's been abused."

His shoulders sag. "Well, if you really think so, maybe you should talk to Shuffle."

I know my VP is right. If Shuffle is half the man I think he is, he'd find the asshat and end his miserable life. Roxie is *his* sister and not my responsibility, and calling him would be the smart thing to do. But I never claimed to be smart.

"Yeah, maybe."

"Screamer, don't."

"Don't what?"

"Don't put this on yourself," he snaps. "You don't even know the girl, and if you're right about her being scared, the last thing she needs is you breathing down her neck like some knight in denim and leather."

"Knight in denim and leather?" I repeat. "Wren's made you all poetic and shit."

He lifts a pen and throws it at me. "Shut the fuck up."

"Look, I'm not gonna do anything stupid," I inform him.

Oh, yeah, you are.

"Pretty sure our definitions of 'stupid' are different."

Without acknowledging his assessment, I head into the back area of the shop. I need to keep my mind and hands busy while I sort through my suspicions about Roxie.

Five and a half hours later, I've finished two jobs and added dozens of questions to the list I have for Shuffle's sister. Journey left an hour ago, and I take my time closing down the shop.

After locking up, I pull my cell from my pocket and send a quick text.

> Me: Meet me at Ballinger's in 30?

I get a reply telling me to make it an hour. Satisfied with that, I ride to the bar. I'm three beers in when the door opens and Shuffle strides in like he owns the joint. Ballinger's is more of a Soulless Kings hangout, but every once in a while, an LTMC member stops by.

"What's wrong?" Shuffle asks as he slides into the booth across from me.

"What makes you think there's something wrong?"

He glares at me. "Because you practically demanded I meet you here."

I take my cell out and pull up the text before turning it so he can see the screen. "I didn't demand. There's a question mark there."

"Cut the shit," he barks. "What's going on? Did something happen with Roxie?"

"What? No, of course not."

"Then why am I here, Screamer?" he demands, his tone impatient.

"Can't a guy just wanna get a drink with a buddy?" When he starts to shift out of the booth, I hold up my hand. "Fine, I'll cut the shit."

"'Bout fuckin' time," he mumbles. "Now, what did you want?"

"Tell me about Roxie," I blurt, and instantly I want to call back the words because Shuffle stiffens and looks like he wants to lunge across the table and strangle the life out of me.

"She's off-limits," he snarls.

"I'm not aski—"

He slams his fist on the table and rises. "Roxie is off-fucking-limits," he repeats as he moves to stand next to where I sit. Wrapping his hand around the back of my neck, he squeezes. "The only thing you need to know about my sister is that I'll gut the next man who hurts her."

With that, he storms out of the bar, leaving me to stare after him. Shuffle gave me nothing while giving me everything, and he doesn't even know it.

I'll gut the next man who hurts her.

So, she *has* been hurt. Now I only need to know two things: Who hurt her, and where the fuck can I find him?

CHAPTER 11
ROXIE

WHAT ABOUT SCREAMER?

"YOU'LL NEVER GUESS WHO I SAW LAST NIGHT."

The excitement in Melody's voice is infectious, and I grin. I haven't spoken to her, Greg, or Sammie since I let them know I arrived at my destination safely. The four of us agreed that I wouldn't tell them where I am, at least for now.

"Who?" I ask.

"Tiffany Smith," she replies, referring to an old coworker of hers who was fired after fucking their boss in the office bathroom.

"No way. Did you talk to her?"

"Hell no. I was leaving a restaurant after dinner with my parents, and she was sitting at a corner table with some poor schmuck."

"Did she see you?"

"Sure did," she confirms. "And girl, if looks could kill."

"I mean, you *are* the one who turned her into HR."

"Only because I was hoping they'd offer me hazard pay for having to hear the noises those two were making," she says with a shudder. "I still don't know how my lunch didn't make a reappearance."

We talk for a few more minutes about the fallout from the report she made, laughing until she suddenly sobers. "Hey, Rox?"

"Yeah?"

"Has Jace tried to get a hold of you?"

Instantly, my good mood vanishes. "No." I don't know why, but that makes me sad and happy at the same time.

"That's good. I talked to Greg yesterday, and he said he saw Jace at the gym." Before I can ask any questions, she continues. "I guess he asked Greg where you are, and when Greg wouldn't tell him, not that he could, Jace threatened him."

"Dammit, Mel, why didn't you lead with this info?" I snap.

"Because you actually sounded happy when you answered," she counters. "I... I didn't want to ruin the mood."

Sighing, I tuck a strand of hair behind my ear. "Yeah, okay. I get it. So, um, what happened when Jace threatened Greg?" I ask, my heart aching for my friend.

She chuckles. "That's the best part. Turns out, an off-duty cop was at the gym and overheard the threat. He escorted Jace to his car, and the gym trespassed him from the property."

"Oh, that's hilarious."

"Even better is that Greg said a few of Jace's buddies were there, too, so I'm sure he was humiliated."

"God, I wish I could've been a fly on the wall."

"Me, too." A beep sounds in the background, and she says, "Oh, hey. That's my door buzzer. Gotta go."

"Okay. Thanks for calling."

"Talk soon?"

"Absolutely."

I disconnect the call and lean against my headboard. When Melody called, I'd been about to head out to the main area of the clubhouse for a drink, but I need a few minutes to myself to process what she told me.

When she asked me if I'd heard from Jace, I'd told the truth. But what I didn't do was remind her that I bought a new phone and got a new number. I didn't expect to hear from him. At least not yet.

I know exactly why that makes me happy, but I wasn't expecting to feel even an ounce of sadness.

He was your fiancé.

Upcoming nuptials or not, the man beat me. Maybe not throughout our entire relationship, but once is enough.

Right?

Right. If I'm being honest with myself, I should've left a lot earlier than I did. Pride and stubbornness are two qualities that have always gotten the best of me.

As for Jace asking Greg where I am... Well, that's exactly why my friends don't know.

But they know about Marble Falls and Shuffle.

Be that as it may, they don't know that this is specifically where I landed.

A knock on my door pulls me from my thoughts, and I stiffen at the sound. Forcing myself to relax, I get to my feet.

"Who is it?"

"Open up, Rox," a feminine voice calls. *Rae.* "You've been cooped up in here all week, and I'm here to see that that changes."

I open my door, and Rae sways on her feet. "Did Shuffle put you up to this?"

She snorts, then burps, which tells me she's drunk. "I don't answer to your brother. Saint's the only man who gets to order me around." She leans in close, cupping her hands over her mouth. "And between you and me, I like it when he gets all bossy."

I grin. "I'm sure you do."

Rae and Saint weren't hitched when I left, but they've been together for as long as I can remember. Rae and I were close growing up, but when I left Marble Falls, the friendship fizzled.

She grabs my arm and drags me into the hall. "C'mon. I've missed you, and I'm done waiting for you to crawl out of your hole."

I want to argue with her, demand she let me go and continue wallowing, but she's right. If I want to avoid questions from my brother and the others, I can't stay in my room forever. It's bad enough that it's been a week since he took me to the shop. I've managed to dodge his inquisition, but he won't hold back forever.

"I'm coming," I say, laughing as she trips over her own two feet, and I have to steady her. "Where's the fire?"

Rae stops in her tracks and looks at me with a serious expression. "If you're lucky, maybe it'll be in your pants later."

"Jesus, Rae. Who the fuck would that even happen with? Huh?"

"You've been gone a while, babe. Plenty of new dick."

"I've been here a little over a week and haven't seen—"

"Please don't finish that fuckin' sentence."

Rae and I both jump at my brother's intrusion. "Eavesdropping will get you nowhere," she sasses.

"And orchestrating a fuckfest for my baby sister will get you into trouble," he retorts, arms crossed over his chest.

"Oh. My. God," I bite out. "First of all, I'm not a baby. You're only five years older than me. And second, I'll fuck whoever I want to fuck."

"The hell you will," he scoffs. "Over my dead body will you cozy up to one of my brothers."

What about Screamer?

The thought pops into my head unbidden, and heat creeps into my cheeks.

"Oh, oh, oh!" Rae exclaims. "You've already got someone in mind, don't you, you slut?"

Shuffle covers his ears and starts humming as he walks away. Rae's grin is devilish.

"You're insane," I accuse playfully. "You know that, right?"

"I don't care. You know *that*, right?"

"I do." I slide my arm through hers. "How 'bout a drink?"

She throws her head back dramatically. "I thought you'd never ask."

Three shots and two beers later, and I'm feeling pretty damn good. Or I was until the 'plenty of new dick' Rae mentioned walks in. The usual crowd has thinned, other than Saint, and has been replaced with men who range in age and looks. Unfortunately, I find myself comparing them to Screamer, which is ridiculous because I don't even know the man other than to know he scares me.

"Hey, gorgeous," one of the bikers says as he sidles up next to me at the bar. "Haven't seen you here before."

Rae, the lady that she is, snorts for what has to be the hundredth time tonight. "Oh, boy," she mutters before downing the shot Saint just set in front of her.

The alcohol in my system bolsters my confidence, so I straighten and face him. "Then you haven't been looking hard enough."

That's true, to an extent. I may not have physically been here for a few years, but there are pictures of me with Shuffle and the rest of the brothers all over the place. If he's spent any amount of time in the clubhouse, and his prospect patch tells me he has, he should know who I am.

That and the fact that I know Shuffle sent out a text to the entire club announcing my arrival and to pronounce me off-limits. I know because he made a point of showing me.

"Baby, I've been looking for you forever," he says, his eyes heavy with lust.

Now it's my turn to snort. "That's the best you can come up with?"

A second prospect joins him, wrapping an arm around his shoulders. "Give him a break, sweet cheeks. Seth's still learning."

I turn to Rae. "Is my name Baby?"

She grins. "No."

"Sweet cheeks?"

"Nope."

"Huh. Then what *is* my name?"

"Like, your legal name or what most people around here know you as?"

"Either works," I tell her, and I hear Saint failing to hold in his laughter at the entire exchange.

"Well," she begins, tapping her head like she has to think. "Your legal name is Roxanne Lynn Allen. And wha—"

"Wait... Did you say Allen?" Seth's face turns ashen.

"And what people around here know you as is Shuffle's sister," Rae finishes as if she hadn't been interrupted.

"Aw, fuck, man," Seth's friend whines.

I smile sweetly at the two men. "Any other questions?"

Seth's expression shifts in a split second, and rage enters his eyes. "You set me up."

"Set you up? How the fuck did I do that?"

He looks from me to Saint. "This is some sort of test, right? It's gotta be a test."

"No test," Saint replies. "But if it were…" He whistles. "Man, you failed miserably."

Seth returns his attention to me. "You stupid bitch," he seethes, grabbing my arm and yanking me toward him.

That's all it takes for me to go from alcohol-induced confidence to terrified. I don't get the chance to pull away or yell because Saint is across the bar so fast, knocking Seth to his ass.

"I'm gonna go get Shuffle," Rae announces from behind me.

"You just fucked up in epic fashion," Saint grunts between punches.

"I had nothing to do with it," Seth's friend insists.

The noise in the room fills my ears, and my limbs begin to shake. I'm transported back to my last night with Jace, and when my knees buckle and my vision darkens, I collapse on the floor.

CHAPTER 12
SCREAMER

There's only one woman who can get the job done.

Tuning out the music penetrating my bedroom walls, I strip out of my greasy clothes and stride into the en suite bathroom to shower. I put in another long day at the shop, longer than usual, and all I want to do is wash the grime from my body and have a few drinks before crashing.

As I let the hot water cascade over my head, my thoughts return to the same thing they have all week: Roxie. I've told myself time and time again that thinking about her, daydreaming about her, will only get me into trouble. But my brain doesn't seem to give a shit.

Neither does your cock.

When an image of her flashes, I'm instantly hard.

Doing my best to ignore my raging boner, I force myself to focus on getting clean, and before getting out to dry, I turn the water to cold and stand there for a few minutes and wait for my lust to wane.

It doesn't happen, but I refuse to rub one out for the seventh day in a row.

Ten minutes later, I'm walking into the main area of the clubhouse, heading straight for the bar. There isn't a party or anything tonight, so it's mostly club members, Bangin' Betties, and old ladies filling the room, and there are several prospects as well.

"Hey, brother," Tracer greets when I slide onto the stool next to him.

I grunt in response.

"What can I get ya?" Braydon, the prospect behind the bar, asks.

"As long as it's cold, I don't really care."

"Rough day?" Tracer asks while Braydon snags a bottle of Perpetual Peace from the cooler and hands it to me.

"You could say that," I mumble.

"Anything I can do?"

I glare at the prospect and tip my head to indicate that he should walk away before answering Tracer. Once we're alone, I say, "Maybe."

"Name it."

Don't do it. It's wrong. Don't, don't, don't.

"I need you to do some digging for me," I tell him.

And you're doing it.

"Diggin' is what I do best," Tracer announces proudly. "Well, that and bustin' heads. Oh, and pussy. I do pussy real fuckin' good, too."

Laughing, I shake my head at him. "How 'bout we stick to the digging?"

He grins with a shrug. "Sure, no problem. Whaddya need me to dig into?"

"Not a what. A who."

"Even better." He downs what remains of his beer and knocks the glass on the bar top to get Braydon's attention. Once he has a fresh brew, he asks, "So, who am I getting all the nitty gritty on?"

I hesitate, berating myself for what I'm about to do, but I know my mind is already made up, so I blurt, "Name's Roxie."

"Roxie, huh?"

"Yep." I take a long pull from my beer. "She's Shuffle's little sister."

Tracer blanches. "Shuffle, as in the president of Limitless Throttle MC?"

"The one and only."

"Damn, man, that's ballsy. What did she do… turn ya down or something?"

"Or something."

"Ooookay." He draws out the word. "You know if I do this and get caught, Shuffle's gonna end me, right? Not to mention the potential shitstorm this could bring between our clubs."

"I do," I confirm. "And I'm asking you anyway. Besides, you won't get caught."

Tracer blows out a breath and takes a drink. "You're right, I won't, but still."

"Will you do it or not?" I bark, getting impatient.

"Of course, I will. But it's gonna cost ya."

"What do you want?"

He takes his time responding, and I clench my jaw while I wait. "Free tune-up on my bike."

"That's..." I shake my head. "Journey and I already do that for all the brothers."

"That's my price."

"Done."

"Good. Now, what do you want to know about this Roxie chick?"

Everything.

"Whatever you can find."

"And when do you want this done by?"

"Yesterday."

Tracer laughs. "Got it. Gimme twenty-four hours."

"You got it. Oh, and one more thing."

Narrowing his eyes, he asks, "What?"

"Let's keep this between us."

"I figured."

"Thanks, T."

"No problem." He polishes off the rest of his beer, stands, and turns to face the rest of the room. I follow his gaze and laugh when I see where it's landed. "Looks like I've got some other business to attend to."

I watch as he saunters toward Molly. When he reaches her, she smiles at him and drags her fingers down his chest. It won't be long before he's got her on her knees, sucking his dick.

Movement catches my attention, and I inwardly groan when I spot Sunny, another Bangin' Betty, sashaying in my direction. Grabbing my beer, I rise to my feet and turn my back on her to go to my room.

There's no doubt in my mind that I need to get laid, but there's only one woman who can get the job done.

And she's as skittish as a newborn colt and as forbidden as the apple in the Garden of Eden.

CHAPTER 13
ROXIE

I don't need a man. I don't want a man.

Beep. Beep. Beep.

My alarm blares, and I groan as I roll over to turn it off. I don't remember setting it, but if the killer headache throbbing at my temples is any indication, I got pretty drunk last night, so my lack of memory isn't surprising.

"Rise and shine, Rox!"

Shuffle strides into my room, not bothering to knock. His cheerful demeanor grates on my nerves, and the smirk on his face tells me he knows exactly what he's doing.

"Jesus, tone it down a bit," I grumble, falling back into the mattress and pulling the covers over my head.

The comforter is yanked away, and my brother leans over me. "Not happening. Get up," he demands.

So much for cheerful.

"Make me," I counter, trying really hard to use my words and not choose violence.

Unfortunately, he has no such problem. He grips my arm and pulls me to my feet. Then he drags me to the attached bath and practically shoves me inside.

"Get a shower," he orders. "I'll have some Tylenol waiting for you when you're done."

With that, he storms out of my room. I want to shout at him to leave me alone, to stop treating me like I'm one of his prospects that he can boss around, but that will only end up with my head splitting all the way in two.

"Fucking asshole," I gripe as I strip and get into the shower.

The warm water helps to clear my head, and memories from the night before come crashing in.

Shit.

Shuffle no doubt wants answers. All I know is that I was having fun with Rae, drinking and catching up, and then Seth and his friend interrupted. Seth crossed a line with me and got his ass beat for his trouble. The last thing I remember is feeling scared and sick to my stomach.

I scrub soap over my skin, wincing when I hit a tender spot on my hip. I glance down and see a large bruise, which reminds me of the fact that I passed out in the main room.

Did Shuffle see that? Is that what has him in a mood?

Only one way to find out.

After getting out of the shower, I dry off, get dressed, and run a comb through my wet hair. I don't bother with makeup because there's no point. I'm not here to impress anyone.

Leaving my room, I go in search of my brother. I find him sitting at one of the tables in the common area, and when he sees me, he stands and closes the distance between us.

"Follow me," he says as he walks past me toward the hallway.

I do as ordered, and we enter his room. "You said you'd have Tylenol," I remind him.

He grabs a bottle of pain reliever off of his dresser and tosses it to me. Next, he snags a bottle of water from his mini fridge and tosses it as well.

"Sit," he commands after I down the pills, pointing at his bed.

"I think I'll stand."

"Sit the fuck down, Rox."

"Sit the fuck down, Rox," I mimic snarkily but do as I'm told.

My brother begins to pace the length of his room, his riding boots thudding on the floor. With each step he takes, I grow uneasy. It's clear he's pissed, but it's not clear why he's taking it out on me.

"What the hell happened last night?" he finally asks.

I huff out a breath. "Like Saint didn't already fill you in."

He whirls on me. "I want to hear your version."

"My version?" I practically screech, and instantly regret it when my head threatens to explode.

"Yeah, your version."

"I got drunk, that Seth jackoff hit on me, Rae and I put him in his place, and he got mean. Saint jumped in and took care of it."

Shuffle glares at me. "You're leaving out the most important part."

I tilt my head, feigning ignorance. "Oh yeah? What's that?"

"You passed the fuck out, Rox," he bellows, throwing his arms in the air. "And that was after you started shaking like a leaf. What gives?"

Absently, I rub my hip where I've got the evidence of what he's asking about. "I was drunk, Ry."

"Right, but in all the times I've gotten wasted with you, you've never passed out. And being drunk doesn't explain the blatant fear I saw on your face after Rae came and got me."

"You sure you weren't drunk? Or high? Because I think you were seeing things."

"Dammit, Rox," he snaps. "Something is going on with you, and I need to know what it is."

I shoot to my feet, anger surging in my veins. "No, Ry, you don't *need* to know. You *want* to know. There's a difference."

"So you don't deny it?"

"Deny what?"

"That there's something going on, something you're not telling me."

Done with this conversation, I storm to the door. "Leave it alone," I warn before walking out of the room.

I quickly get my jacket, cross-body bag, and cell from my own room and leave the clubhouse.

The cool air causes goosebumps to break out over my flesh, but I ignore it. I have to get the hell out of here before I do or say something I can't take back.

With no destination in mind, I ride aimlessly for an hour or so. Eventually, I find myself parking at the curb in front of the bike shop. Before I can give it a second thought, I go inside, and the little bell dings with my entrance.

"Someone will be with you in a minute," a man calls from the back area.

I don't recognize the voice, and disappointment settles over me. "No hurry," I call back.

Ten seconds later, Screamer comes through the swinging door and grins. "I thought that was your voice."

Instinctually, I take a step back. "Oh, I, um…" *Get your shit together, Roxie.* "Yeah, it's me," I say lamely.

"You okay?" he asks, and the genuine concern I see in his eyes is almost my undoing.

"Fine," I lie. "I just…"

"You just what?"

I push past the fear because, really, what the fuck am I afraid of? This man has done nothing wrong.

"I brought my bike," I blurt, hitching a thumb over my shoulder.

His eyes light up with amusement, and he smiles. "I see that."

"Shuffle says you're the best."

Screamer leans his forearms on the counter and assesses me. "Did he?"

Swallowing, I nod. "Yep."

"I'm the best at a lot of things. Did he happen to specify?"

"Bikes. Mechanics. He said you're the best at that."

Fuck, I sound like an idiot.

"What else did Shuffle say about me?"

"I, um… nothing, why?" I ask, unease in my tone.

"Funny. He hasn't told me anything about you either."

"Nothing to tell."

He chuckles. "Oh, I doubt that, sweetheart. I have a feeling there's a whole lot about you that someone could tell."

Lowering my eyes, I stare at the floor. There is, but I find myself wanting Screamer to work for the information, prove that he wants it, and not because it's simply handed to him on a silver platter.

"Look, do you wanna work on my bike or not?" I finally ask.

He straightens. "Sure. You actually gonna leave it this time?"

"Yeah, but…"

"But what?" he asks when I go silent.

I take a deep breath as I lift my gaze and lock eyes with him. Forcing the words out of my mouth, I say, "I didn't exactly think this through. I'll need a ride home."

We stare at each other for a long minute, and my

core tightens. God, he's hot. Hot and a biker. And a man. I don't need a man. I don't want a man.

But you want him.

"Yo, Journey, I'll be back," Screamer shouts before walking around the counter. "C'mon, sweetheart. I'll take you home."

CHAPTER 14
SCREAMER

So am I, sweetheart.

I KEEP SNEAKING GLANCES AT ROXIE AS I DRIVE HER home. She's leaning her head against the glass, staring out the window at the scenery we pass. When I opened the passenger door to the truck, she seemed shocked that I wasn't taking her on my bike. I may be an idiot, but I'm not stupid. Putting her on the back of my Harley would have sent a message I'm not ready to send, and she's not ready to receive.

"You hungry?" I ask, desperate to fill the silence.

She stiffens at the sound of my voice, and I watch as she takes a deep breath, forcing her shoulders to relax.

"I could eat," she admits as she slowly turns to face me.

I'm surprised by her response but pleased. "Good because I'm starving."

She drags her eyes from my face to my chest to my stomach and then lower before raising it again. "You hardly look like you're starving."

My cock throbs behind my jeans. Not just at the double meaning in her comment, but also at the sass in her voice. I much prefer my women with a bit of attitude.

"Like what you see?" I tease. A blush stains her cheeks, and I grin. "I'll take that as a yes."

Roxie twists to stare out the window again. "I'll eat at home."

"Aw, c'mon," I plead. "I didn't mean anything by it."

She huffs out a laugh. "Right. You're all the same."

"All?"

"Bikers," she responds simply. "Men."

It's my turn to stiffen. "Not all men are the same," I say quietly.

She whips her head in my direction, staring at me as if silently willing me to explain, but I don't. If she wants to know something, she's going to have to use her words and ask me.

"Is the diner still on the other side of town?" Roxie asks after a beat.

Flexing my fingers on the steering wheel, I nod. "Yep. That sound good to you?"

"Yes."

I pull a U-turn at the next traffic light. If Roxie wants diner food, she'll get diner food. Five minutes later, I'm parking, and she's hopping out of the truck.

"Next time, let me get your door," I state when I walk around the front of the vehicle.

"Next time?"

Rather than answer, I reach for her hand without thinking, and she jerks away from me. I put a little space between us, not wanting to spook her. I might not have seen the signs with my sister, but they're flashing in bright neon with Roxie.

A waitress leads us to a table tucked into a corner, but after we sit, she doesn't retreat. Instead, she stands next to my chair and stares at me with appreciation.

"Seriously?" Roxie snaps. "You do see me here, right?"

The waitress clears her throat and looks at my dining partner. "Yeah, I see you. Sorry. I, um… I'm Jenny, and I'll be taking care of you today."

"Respectfully, no, you won't," I tell her, and her eyes widen. "Is Kate working today?"

"Kate?"

"Did I stutter?"

"N-no, sir," Jenny babbles. "I'll, uh… I'll go get Kate, and she can take care of you."

"Thank you, Jenny."

"You didn't have to do that," Roxie hisses when Jenny walks away.

"I beg to differ."

"But… why?"

"Because she was disrespectful to you, and I'm here with you."

"But we're not together."

Shrugging, I reply, "Maybe not, but I'm still here with you, sweetheart. And Jenny doesn't know that we're not a couple."

Roxie leans back in her chair. "You're—"

"Not like all other men." I grab two menus from the holder and hand her one. "Any clue what you want?"

Returning the menu to its rightful place, she nods. "Burger, fries, and a milkshake."

I clap my own menu closed. "That sounds good. I think I'll have the same."

Kate comes to the table and takes our orders. We exchange polite chit chat for a few minutes, and she includes Roxie. Once we're alone again, Roxie glances around the diner as if to make sure she knows exactly what's going on around her.

The door opens, and a man walks in. He hesitates

at the entrance for a moment before Jenny escorts him to a table on the other side of the restaurant. The guy is wearing a white Polo shirt with black trousers, and his shoes alone would give him away as an outsider, but it's the way he carries himself that rubs me the wrong way. I shift my eyes from them to Roxie, and her face is pale as she looks at me.

That's not good.

For a brief moment, I wonder if that's the guy who hurt her, but I dismiss it. No way a guy would be stupid enough to show his face in Marble Falls. Shuffle would kill him… if he knows what happened.

"Everything okay?" I ask. "You look like you've seen a ghost."

She's quiet for a second, and then she stands. "I gotta go."

I jump to my feet and grab her arm, ignoring the way she struggles against my hold. "Wait a sec," I demand, my eyes darting to the man who entered and back again. "Do you know him?"

She frantically shakes her head. "N-no. He, uh, reminds me of someone, that's all."

"Okay." I try to urge her back into her chair, but she stands firm. "Can I at least get our food to go?" I ask.

"I don't care. I just have to get out of here."

"Okay, okay. Then we'll get out of here." We move through the diner to the front counter. "Hey, Kate," I say. "Can you make our orders to go?"

"Sure thing, Ben."

Roxie tips her head back and arches a brow. "Ben?"

I smirk. "What? Did you really think Screamer is my real name?"

"Well, no, of course not. I know it's a road name."

"Look, not many people can get away with calling me Ben," I admit. "Not since…"

"Not since what?" she prompts, seemingly having forgotten the man who scared her.

"Nothing." I don't want to talk about Ally, about my parents.

Just then Kate sets a bag of food on the counter. I pay the tab, and we walk outside to the truck.

"I'll show you mine if you show me yours," Roxie says as she puts her seatbelt on.

I choke on the sip of milkshake I'm taking. "W-what?" I sputter.

She rolls her eyes. "Not like that."

"I'm afraid you're gonna have to clarify because now all I can think about is us showing each other our naughty parts."

"Naughty parts? What are you, eight?" she asks, then takes a sip of her milkshake.

"Eight inches, yeah."

It's her turn to choke, and it takes several minutes for her to gain her composure. "Jesus, are you always this way?"

"Does it matter? You seem to have forgotten whatever it was that spooked you."

Instantly, her good mood vanishes, and she becomes rigid in the passenger seat. "I'd like to go home now."

"What about your proposition?"

"Dammit, Screamer, be serious. I'm done joking around."

"So am I, sweetheart. So am I."

CHAPTER 15
ROXIE

HE LOST THAT RIGHT THE SECOND HE TRIED TO BREAK ME.

"Remember when I said not all men are the same?"

Screamer and I are sitting at a picnic table at the park. It's mid-day, so the place is empty, leaving us to talk about whatever we want with no distractions. I'm not entirely certain this is a good idea, but I refuse to let my fear win out.

"It was, like, less than an hour ago, so yeah."

We each take a few bites of our food, and he seems to be trying to find the words to explain. Eventually, he sets his half-eaten burger down and levels his gaze on mine.

"I had an older sister, Ally," he begins. "She was, hands down, the best big sister I could've asked for. She wasn't like a lot of older siblings, ya know?" The question is rhetorical, and he continues. "Ally always included me when she hung out with her friends. I adored her, and I knew the feeling was mutual. We were nine years apart, but she didn't treat me like I was a pesky baby brother. Even when she went off to college, she would let me visit some weekends, or she'd come home to spend time with me."

When he stops to eat some fries, I say, "She sounds amazing."

He gets a faraway look in his eyes and stares off into space. "She was. Then she met Brian. I still remember when she brought him home to meet our parents."

"You don't have to tell me," I say, his pain washing over me to mix with my own.

Screamer whips his eyes to mine. "Yeah, I do."

"Okay."

He takes a deep breath. "Brian was great at first. Our parents seemed to like him, and when Ally married him, I was excited because I was getting a brother. But after the wedding, everything changed. Ally stopped coming around as much, stopped calling and texting. Family dinners were somber because she always found a reason to back out. Mom and Dad were worried about her, and so was I." Screamer scrubs his hands over his face. "When my dad and I finished fixing up his old Harley, I made the two-hour drive to see her, to confront her about what was going on with her. At first, she didn't want to let me in the door, but I forced my way into the house." After blowing out a breath, he continues. "Fuck, Roxie, the bruises. She'd tried to cover them with makeup and certain clothes, but I saw them." At this admission, I cringe, knowing I'd done exactly the same thing. "I begged her to leave with me. For hours, I pleaded, but she refused. She kept insisting that Brian hadn't meant to hurt her. Fucking hell, she was so brainwashed, conditioned to believe the best of him and the worst of herself and everyone else."

I got lucky.

As he talks, all I can think is that I got lucky. Jace was an asshole, and yes, he hurt me badly, but I got out. I left, and I'm alive because of it.

"What happened to Ally?" I ask when he goes quiet.

"I was eighteen, and she'd promised me she'd come see me for my birthday. When she didn't show, my parents suggested we go see her." He shrugs like none of this is a big deal, but his eyes shine with unshed tears. "I was mad that she didn't come, so I chose to stay home and prepare for the date I had the next day. I needed condoms of all things." Waving his hand dismissively, he goes on. "Anyway, the best the police were able to piece together is that

Brian had murdered Ally and was trying to clean up the crime scene when my parents got there. He killed them so there wouldn't be any witnesses. I'm sure he would've come for me next, but the neighbors heard my mom's screams when she saw Ally's body and called nine-one-one. Cops picked him up that night."

"Good," I say vehemently. "At least the bastard is behind bars."

"Fucker's six feet under."

"Oh. Well, even better," I tell him honestly.

"I killed him," he admits, and I should be surprised, but I'm not. "He was deemed incompetent to stand trial and admitted to a state mental institution. Soulless Kings helped me break him out, and I took his life the same way he took Ally's, took my parent's." Screamer reaches across the picnic table and grabs my hand before I can pull away. "I meant what I said, Roxie. Not all men are the same. I'm nothing like Brian. I'd never hurt a woman, never lay a finger on one. But I am like him in one crucial way... I'm a murderer."

My mind tumbles over his words in an effort to read between the lines. But there are no lines. He's baring his soul to me, admitting his flaws, his sins. While I don't condone violence, don't agree with vigilante justice or biker justice, I get it. Someone had to make Brian pay for his crime, and unfortunately, that someone was Screamer. The system failed him.

"I'm sorry you had to go through all of that."

"That's just it, sweetheart. I don't want your sympathy. I told you because I want you to know that you might be able to hide whatever happened from your brother, but I see more than most. I've made it my life's purpose to see what others don't."

"I…" I pull my hand out of his and rest it in my lap. "I don't know what you're talking about."

"I showed you mine," he says. "Time to show me yours." Screamer softens his tone with a smile, and I find myself wanting to tell him. "Besides, if you don't tell me, I've got other ways to find out what I want to know."

"Let me guess… your club's tech guy?"

"Honestly, I'm surprised Shuffle hasn't had LTMC's techie do some digging."

"He knows I'd kill him if he did. My brother may be oblivious and an asshole, but I know he loves me in his own way. He's just more focused on the club, which has worked to my advantage."

"Still, I don't get how he didn't pick up on the broken ribs, the yellowish tint under your makeup, the timidness you've displayed despite being raised around bikers."

My eyes widen. "How… How'd you know?"

"Like I said, I see more than most. So, care to enlighten me?" When I don't say anything, he asks, "Did you know the man in the diner?"

"What?"

"The man in the diner, the one dressed like a pussy. He came in, and your entire demeanor changed."

"Oh, um…" I shake my head. "No. He just reminded me of someone."

That's not entirely true. Yes, the guy reminded me of Jace, so much so that I can't be sure it wasn't him. And if it was? Well, that's a problem for some other time, like when I'm not with Screamer.

"Okay." The way he says the word, it's clear he's not sure whether to believe me. "So, he reminded you of the guy who broke your ribs."

I nod and take several calming breaths. "Growing up, I always knew I wanted to leave Marble Falls. I was tired of living around the biker lifestyle and needed to see what else the world has to offer." Realizing how that sounds, I add, "No offense."

"None taken."

I smile gratefully. "Anyway, I moved across the country, to the east coast. I got a job, made friends, met a guy. All the normal things people do at my age. Jace was everything I thought I wanted, the exact opposite of a biker. Again, no offense."

He chuckles. "Sweetheart, you're here with me, not him. No offense taken."

"Right. So, things with Jace were great. Then he proposed, and he changed. I should be planning my wedding, but instead, I'm here, hiding."

"I'd say you're here to heal not hide."

"Maybe, but it doesn't change the facts. I fell for a man who made me a fool. He became controlling and mean. It was little things at first. He didn't like a shirt I was wearing or the color of my nail polish. Then it turned into him not liking my friends and the time I spent with them or the phone calls with my brother. I thought he just loved me, ya know? I thought he wanted me all to himself but in a good way. I grew up around possessive men, so I brushed it off."

"There's a difference between being possessive and being controlling," he says. "If you were mine, I'd be possessive as hell, but that doesn't mean I'd tell you how to act or what to wear or who to be friends with."

"What does it mean?" I ask, suddenly needing to know.

"It means you'd belong to me. I'd protect you with my life, love you with everything I have, and take care of you so that you want for nothing."

"Does that go both ways?"

"What do you mean?"

"What if I was possessive of you? Would that piss you off?"

Screamer grins widely. "Fuck, no, sweetheart. If I'm with a woman, if we're committed to each other, that protection, that love and care… it better go both ways."

I tuck a strand of hair behind my ear. "Good to know."

"But we're not talking about a relationship between us. I want to hear the rest of your story."

The fact that he's not focusing on what could be between us or making any move to hit on me or get in my pants lights me up from the inside out. He genuinely seems interested in me as a person, and that's what I crave right now.

Well, that and his dick.

Shaking that thought away, I dive into the last night I was with Jace. "We had a dinner party. Some of Jace's colleagues and friends were at the house. Everything went off without a hitch, or so I thought. When everyone left, he went off on me, accusing me of looking at a male friend of his too much and all sorts of things. He became physical. I managed to get away and to our bedroom, but it did me no good." Wringing my hands in my lap, I fight off tears. "He beat the shit out of me that night and then left me there to bleed. I got to my cell and texted my friends. They came right away and helped me pack up and get the fuck out."

"Good friends."

"The best. When I left, I got a rental car under a different name and slowly made my way to Marble Falls. It took me two weeks because I wanted to heal as much as I could before facing my brother. I also dumped my cell and got a new one with a new number. Obviously, the wedding's off, although I never officially told him that."

"You leaving should be enough for him to get the picture."

"You'd think. He confronted my friend, Greg, at the gym about where I am. Greg, Sammie, and Melody don't know I'm here, so even if he could get them to talk, there's nothing they can tell him."

"Smart."

"I just…" I huff out a breath. "I just wish I'd been smart sooner, ya know?"

"I do, but you can't put that on yourself. You were being abused. Maybe not physically at first, but he manipulated you. You got out when it counted."

"I guess." I look into his eyes. "So, I showed you mine. And now I need a favor."

"I'm not gonna tell your brother."

Relief whooshes out of me in a long exhale. "Thank you. I know I should, but I can't face his judgment."

"I might not know Shuffle well, but our clubs do work together on occasion. I don't think you're giving him enough credit."

"Trust me, he'll judge. Maybe not me specifically, but he was never on board with my decision to leave and giving him a reason to say, 'I told you so' is the last thing I can deal with."

"Okay. I won't tell him. But please think about clueing him in if for no other reason than it wouldn't hurt to have him watching your back."

Instantly, I bristle. "I don't need him to watch my back. I'm a grown ass woman and can take care of myself."

Screamer holds his hands up in surrender. "Whoa, Roxie, I didn't mean to imply that you can't. Shit, I'm all for you being an independent badass, but what's the point in having an MC in your corner if you don't use it to your advantage?"

He has a point, and it's a big reason I came back here, but that doesn't mean I'm going to admit it.

"I'm ready to go home," I say, standing and gathering my trash.

He sighs. "Yeah, okay."

We toss our garbage in a can on the way to the truck, and he opens my door for me, being the perfect gentleman. It simultaneously grates on my nerves and warms my heart. When he pulls up to the LTMC clubhouse, the prospect from last night is at the gate.

"Hey, Screamer." He ducks his head to look at me. "Hi, Roxie. I don't think we were actually introduced last night, but I'm Mark. Really sorry about Seth."

Screamer glances at me with questions in his eyes, but I ignore him. "Wasn't your fault, Mark. Can you just buzz us in, please?"

"Sure thing."

The gate opens, and a minute later, the truck is in park in the gravel lot in front of the clubhouse. I take off my seat belt and open the door, but Screamer gently grabs my arm, forcing me to turn and look at him.

"What?" I ask.

He opens the center console and snags a pen and napkin. After writing something down, he hands the napkin to me. "Here's my number. Ya know, in case you ever need anything."

"Oh. Thanks."

"Roxie?"

"Yeah?"

"I'll give you a call when your bike is ready to be picked up."

I smack my forehead with my free hand. "Shit, I guess you need my number, too."

He laughs at that. "It's in the shop's system from when you came in the first time."

"And let me guess... even if it wasn't, you have your ways of finding it?"

Screamer winks. "You got it."

"Well, thank you for the food."

"Anytime."

"See ya."

I shut the passenger door behind me and stride to the clubhouse entrance. As soon as I step inside, my phone vibrates in my pocket. I ignore it, thinking it's Screamer who I'm sure put my number in his contacts as soon as he could.

My room is quiet, and as I set my cross-body on the bench at the foot of my bed, my phone vibrates again, and then again.

"Geez, chill," I mutter when I pull it out of my pocket.

My entire body seizes when I see the number that accompanies the texts. It's not a saved number, but I'd recognize it anywhere: Jace.

> Jace: You're really letting yourself go, Roxie. That'll have to change when we get back home.
>
> Jace: Leaving me was a mistake. Shacking up with a Texas hick is just the icing on the cake. You'll pay for that.
>
> Jace: Ignoring me isn't going to make me go away.

I throw my cell onto the bed and curl up on top of the comforter in the fetal position. How did he get my new number? Was that really him at the diner? And more importantly, how the fuck is he going to make me pay?

As I play different scenarios in my head, my phone buzzes with a notification. Fear races through me, and I want to ignore it, but I don't. Jace doesn't get to have that kind of power over me anymore.

The screen is lit up, and I silently thank God when it's a different number.

> Unknown: This is Screamer, or Ben if you'd prefer. I meant what I said... call me if you need anything. And Roxie?
>
> Me: What?

> Screamer: Thanks for listening today. It's been a long time since I've talked about Ally, and it felt good.

I lower my phone and smile. No, Jace doesn't get to have power over me. He lost that right the second he tried to break me.

CHAPTER 16
SCREAMER

I AM FUCKED.

"I'M GONNA GIVE ROXIE A CALL AN—"

"I'll call her," I bark, narrowing my eyes on Journey.

He smirks. "Oh, damn, it's like that, is it?"

"Like what?"

It's been a few days since I gave Roxie my cell number, and she has yet to use it. Hell, she didn't even text me back. I'm dying to talk to her, but I know I've gotta let her do things in her own time. Calling her to let her know her bike is ready is a different matter. That's not a social call. It's business.

That's what I'm telling myself anyway.

"You like her," he says simply.

"She's easy to like."

"I'm not talking platonically, and you know it."

I smack him upside the head before taking my cell out of my pocket. "Leave it alone."

Pulling up her contact info, I hit send and press the phone to my ear.

"Screamer and Roxie sitting in a tree, K-I-S-S-I-N-G," Journey sings.

"Shut the fuck up," I snap.

"Excuse me," Roxie says.

"Shit, sorry. Not you, sweetheart."

"Sweetheart?" Journey mouths silently.

I flip him off and focus on my phone call. "How ya doin', Roxie?"

"I'm good. My bike done?"

"Yep. I was thinking I could bring it to you when I'm done here at the shop."

"Ah, no, that's okay. I'll just have one of the brothers give me a ride."

I bristle at the thought of her on the back of another man's bike. "No."

"No?"

Dammit, one word is going to be my downfall, I just know it. "I, uh… Isn't there an old lady or club whore who can bring you?"

"There are, but I'd rather ride."

"And I'd rather you not be on the back of another bike. You know what that symbolizes."

"I'm just gonna go grab you a shovel," Journey comments. "Make it easier to bury yourself."

"Fuck off," I bark.

"Screamer," Roxie snaps. "If you're gonna be on the phone with me, talk to me, not whoever the fuck is there."

"It's Journey, and he's being a dick."

"I don't care if it's Jesus Christ himself."

I grin. "Damn, sweetheart. I like this side of you."

There's a long pause, then she inhales. "You do?"

"Absofuckinglutely. You speaking your mind, not taking my shit… It's sexy."

"Oh."

"Anyway, back to you getting a ride."

"Screamer, I grew up around most of these guys. Shit, I've already ridden with the majority of them. It means nothing to me."

"It could to them."

"I highly doubt it. But fine, whatever. I'll have one of them bring me over in the club SUV."

"Thanks, sweetheart."

"I'm not doing it for you. I'm doing it because it's cold out."

"Keep telling yourself that."

"I will."

"See ya when you get here."

I disconnect the call before she can change her mind.

"Yeah, you're fucked. Either you're gonna keep digging yourself holes or you're gonna fall so hard you won't know what hit you."

I glare at Journey, hating that he's right.

I am fucked.

CHAPTER 17
ROXIE

No, no, no!

"Hey, Rox."

I glance around the room until my eyes land on Saint. He's the only one here, which is perfect. He's married, and Rae couldn't care less if I rode on the back of his bike. She knows it means nothing. Screamer, on the other hand... he's gonna learn that he can't tell me what to do.

"Hey. You busy?"

"No, what's up?"

"Would you mind taking me to the shop to pick up my bike?"

"Not at all. Gimme a few minutes to call Rae and let her know where I'll be, and I'll meet you outside."

"Thanks, Saint. I appreciate it."

"No problem, Rox."

Thirty minutes later, he's parking at the curb in front of the shop. When I glance inside, I spot Screamer immediately because he's standing at the front and looking out the window. The glare on his face only makes me laugh.

"What's so funny?" Saint asks as he kicks his leg over the seat and helps me to my feet.

"Oh, you're about to find out."

We walk inside, and Screamer steps in front of Saint. "Aren't you married?" he demands.

Saint's eyes dart from him to me, and he chuckles. "Nice one, Rox."

"What?" I say innocently, batting my eyelashes.

"Calm down there, killer," Saint says to Screamer. "You know I am. Fuck, you know Rae, too. You seriously think I'd put another woman on the back of my bike if my old lady wasn't okay with it?"

Screamer's shoulders slump, and he focuses on me. "You said you'd be coming in the club's SUV."

I open my mouth to respond, but Saint beats me to it. "The SUV wasn't there. It's being used for club business today, so no one could've brought her in it."

"Oh."

"Anyway, I'm outta here," Saint says, turning to the door but pausing his attention on me. "You good here, Rox?"

"I'm not gonna hurt her," Screamer snarls.

"I'm fine, Saint," I say. "I'll see you back at the clubhouse."

He nods once and leaves. After he pulls away, I shift to look at Screamer.

"First off," I begin. "You don't own me, which means you don't get to dictate how I get from point A to point B. Secondly, just because we swapped stories the other day, that doesn't give you license to suddenly get all possessive." He opens his mouth to speak, but I hold up a hand to stop him. "I'm not done. I know you say there's a difference between possessive and controlling, so I'm gonna give you the benefit of the doubt and call your attitude possessive, but make no mistake… it was controlling."

"I'm sorry."

"And furthermore," I say, but then his words register. "What?"

"I'm sorry. You're right."

"I'm… oh. Well, good."

Screamer chuckles and takes a step toward me. "Fuck, you make me crazy." He reaches out to cup my cheek, and when I flinch, he doubles down with both hands on either side of my face. "Ever since you walked in here with your brother, I haven't been able to get you off my mind. Day and night, you're all I think about."

"I'm not looking for a relationship, Screamer. It's only been weeks since I left a toxic one, and I'm not ready."

He rubs his thumbs gently under my eyes. "I know. I'm good with that, really, I am. All I ask is that you keep an open mind, and don't shut me out."

I contemplate what he's asking. I'd be lying if I said I wasn't curious about him, about where this could lead, but I'm definitely not lying about not being ready. Jace ruined me, incinerated my self-confidence, tore down my defenses, and made me unable to trust anyone, myself included.

My gut tells me that everything Screamer has told me is true, that he's different and not at all like Jace or other asshole men. The problem is, my gut told me Jace was good, too.

Keep an open mind, and don't shut me out.

Can I do that? I don't know. But I owe it to myself to try. If I don't, then Jace wins.

"Okay."

"Okay?"

"Yeah. You're gonna have to be patient with me, though."

"Sweetheart, patience is my middle name."

I snort a laugh. "Somehow, I doubt that."

Screamer shrugs. "Okay, so maybe it's not, but I'm willing to give it a shot."

"Fair enough."

"Good." He leans down and kisses my forehead softly before releasing me.

And just like that, I'm a goner. Forehead kisses are my kryptonite. Jace never once did that, which should've been a red flag.

"Gimme a few minutes, and I can follow you home," he says, stepping away from me.

"I'll be fine," I assure him. "I don't need an escort."

"Not saying you do. But I wanna make sure you don't have any problems with your Harley, so please, let me follow you home to make sure you get there safely?"

"Well, when you put it like that…"

Ten minutes later, we're in the back parking lot, starting up our bikes. I lead the way as we head to the LTMC clubhouse. We make it to the outskirts of town, and as soon as we clear the city limits, I open up the throttle and fly, and Screamer right next to me with a giant grin lighting up his face.

There's a fork in the road ahead, about fifteen miles before the clubhouse, and when it comes into view, the sunlight catches on something shiny. I squint, trying to make out what it is, and my stomach bottoms out when I realize what I'm seeing.

Bringing my Harley to a screeching halt, I lower

the kickstand and jump off to scramble to the wreckage and Saint's bloody and broken body.

"No!" I shout, my knees buckling.

Before I can hit the ground, Screamer's there to hold me up. He wraps his arms around me, pulling my back against his chest.

"Shhh," he croons as I wail.

"No, no, no! Not Saint!"

Screamer lowers me to the ground so he can check on my friend. He presses a finger to his throat, and when he finds no pulse, he shakes his head. "I'm so sorry, sweetheart. He's gone."

"Oh my God, this can't be happening. How is this happening?"

I twist and turn to take in our surroundings in an effort to find something, anything, that would explain the scene before me. Nothing jumps out until my eyes land on a piece of paper wedged sticking out from under Saint.

"W-what's that?" I ask, pointing to it.

Screamer yanks the paper out and unfolds it. As he scans the contents, his eyes narrow, and his body becomes rigid.

"Son of a bitch," he seethes.

"What?" I demand, crawling over the gravel toward him. "W-what is it?"

When he hesitates, I snatch it from his hand, but when I read the words, I wish I hadn't.

> *This is what happens when you act like a whore. As if spreading your legs for the Texan hick wasn't bad enough, you had to do the same for a married man. I thought you were better than this, Roxie.*

CHAPTER 18
SCREAMER

He won't get away with this.

"This is all my fault."

After Roxie read the note, she leaned against me, seeking comfort. I'm not sure she realizes she even did it, but I'm not about to point it out. I know we should call the cops, or at the very least, Shuffle, and yet… Here we sit on the side of the road, neither of us taking out our cell phones.

"Stop," I command. "You can't blame yourself."

She pushes away and glares at me over her shoulder. "If not for me, Saint wouldn't be dead. I could've gone anywhere, but I chose to come back to Marble Falls. If I hadn't, Saint would be home, waiting on Rae to get home from work. Pretty sure that's the very definition of being able to blame myself."

Bursting into tears, Roxie tries to stand but can't.

"You didn't cause this wreck," I tell her.

She sniffles. "Jace is here for me. Why didn't he just come for me? First the texts, and now this? What the fuck will he do next?"

"Texts?"

She reaches into her jacket pocket, pulls out her cell, taps on the screen, and then flips it for me to read. "I got them after you dropped me off the other day."

As I read the messages, I see red. "So, it was Jace at the diner," I say matter-of-factly.

"I guess so."

"Why didn't you tell me?"

Roxie blanches at the accusation in my tone. "Because I never thought anything would come of it. I mean, if he was gonna hurt me, wouldn't he do that instead of sending me texts and..." Her eyes fall to Saint. "And this?"

"Jesus fucking Christ, sweetheart," I snap. "He beat you, the one person he should've cherished and treated like a goddamn queen. If he's capable of that, he's capable of anything."

"Don't yell at me," she hisses.

I take a deep breath to calm my emotions. "I'm sorry," I say, getting to my feet and pulling her to hers. "I didn't mean to yell at you."

Roxie brushes dust from her jeans before straightening and wiping the wetness from her face. "I gotta go. I need to call Shuffle, and I need to tell Rae." Her voice cracks, so she takes a deep breath. "The police need to be called so they can investigate. I'm sure I'll need to help plan a funeral. And I should probably call my friends to warn them. If Jace did this, they aren't safe, especially if he finds out they helped me get away. Oh, shit, what if he alre—"

"Roxie!" She presses her lips together at my shout. "What you need to do is slow down and breathe. One thing at a time, okay?" She nods absently. "First, I'm going to text Crow and ask him to have Addison meet us at the Soulless Kings' clubhouse. She's his old lady and the law around here and can help. Then we're going to get the hell out of here. We're sitting ducks out in the open."

"What about Shuffle and Rae?"

"You can call your brother from my place. Right now, I don't think it's a good idea to be near LTMC property. Jace probably already knows the location, and you being there is just inviting trouble."

"You're right," she agrees. "I'm not ready to tell him everything yet, anyway."

"I'm not sure you can keep your secrets for much longer, sweetheart. Not now that a club brother is dead."

Roxie drops her head and stares at the ground. "Saint didn't deserve this."

"No, he didn't. But again, it's not your fault." I put two fingers under her chin and force her to look me in the eyes. "He won't get away with this, I promise."

After a few seconds, she nods, and I lower my arm. Taking my cell out of my cut, I pull up the texting app.

> Me: Meet me at the clubhouse, bring Addi, 911

Almost immediately, my phone pings with a response.

> Crow: Done. Church?

> Me: Definitely

I return my phone to my pocket. "C'mon, Roxie," I say, pulling her attention away from Saint.

"I don't want to leave him," she says, sniffling back tears.

"We don't have a choice. We have to go."

Squaring her shoulders, she turns on her heel and walks to her bike. I follow, and the ride to the clubhouse seems to take an eternity. As soon as she and I step inside, Crow and Addison, his old lady, are there to greet us.

Crow looks down at my hands, and his expression hardens when he sees the blood. "What the fuck happened?"

I glance down. "It's not mine."

"Whose is it?" Addison asks.

"It's Saint's," Roxie replies stoically before I can. "H-he's dead."

"Hey, Ember!" Crow shouts to Ghost's old lady. "Take Roxie and help her get cleaned up."

Ember rushes across the room and smiles at Roxie. "Hi. How 'bout we find you some clean clothes, hmm?"

"Um…" She glances at me as if to ask permission, and when I nod, she continues. "Yeah, okay. But I, um, need to call my brother."

"Let Ember help you first," Crow states, his tone calm. "Then you can call Shuffle."

Ember puts her arm around Roxie and leads her out of the main area. As soon as they're out of sight, I let my rage take over.

"I'm gonna fucking kill him," I snarl.

"Kill who?" my president asks.

"Her fiancé."

Crow sighs. "I have a feeling you've got a lot to

catch us up on. C'mon, we'll talk in church." When I don't follow him, he glances over his shoulder. "She'll be fine, Screamer. Ember's got her."

Forcing myself to regulate my breathing and erratic heartbeat, I jerk a nod.

"She better be."

CHAPTER 19
ROXIE

All hell breaks loose.

"What the fuck do you mean?"

I wince at my brother's words. When I called him a few minutes ago, he asked if he could call me back because he was busy, but I told him no. Shuffle proceeded to argue with me, telling me that whatever it was I needed to talk about could wait. He wouldn't let me get a word in, so I blurted 'Saint's dead', and that shut him up… for a second.

Tears blur my vision, and I wipe them away with the sleeve of the hoodie Ember gave me to wear. "I mean, he's gone, Ry. Screamer and I found him on the side of the road. He, um…" I swallow past the lump in my throat. "He wrecked, I guess, and died."

"You and Screamer?"

"That's what you're focusing on?" I demand, my nerves rattling and anger spiking. "I just told you that one of your club brothers is dead, and you wanna bark in my ear about who was with me when I found him?"

"Where are you now? Still at the scene? I'm gonna come meet you."

"No, Ryan, I'm not there," I say. "I, um… I'm at the Soulless Kings' clubhouse."

"You can't be serious," he seethes.

"I can, and I am. I guess Crow's wife is law enforcement. Screamer is filling her in now, as well as his club."

He says nothing for a minute, and I curl up on the bed. Ember told me this is Screamer's room, and the clothes I'm wearing are his. They're huge on me, but in them, I feel comforted, safe.

"You need to come home, now," my brother orders. "We'll discuss this when you get here."

"I'm not a fucking child," I snap. "And I'm not coming home."

"You'll either come home on your own, or I'll come there and drag your ass out."

I know I should tell him everything and explain to him why leaving here is dangerous. If I opened up to him, he'd back off rather than yell at me. But when

I open my mouth to speak, nothing comes out. The last hour is wreaking havoc on my nerves and emotions, and I'm tired. So goddamn tired.

"Roxie?" His voice comes through the line, and I go rigid. "Get your ass home."

"Ya know what, *Shuffle*?" I sneer his road name in an effort to let him know how I feel about him treating me like one of his club members who he can order around. Passive aggressive? Yes. Do I give a shit? Not at all. "Fuck off."

I disconnect the call and turn my cell off. There's enough going on right now without having to deal with his misogynistic and overbearing attitude.

A knock on the door has me sitting up. "Come in."

Ember steps into the room, and she's carrying a tray. "I brought you something to eat and drink."

"Thanks, but I'm not hungry."

"Well, I'll leave it here in case you change your mind." She sets it on the nightstand and retreats to the door. "Let me know if I can do anything else, okay?"

"I will."

Once I'm alone again, exhaustion tugs at my eyelids. I must doze off because the next thing I know, I'm startled by the sound of shouting.

Jumping off the bed, I rush to the door and open

it a crack. Straining to hear what's going on, I tense when I hear a voice I recognize. I race into the common area, and freeze when I see my brother, Bear, Blush, and Creep trying to push past several Soulless Kings' members.

"What the hell are you doing here?" I hiss after closing the distance between us.

Shuffle glares at me. "I told you I was coming."

"Jesus, you can't do this!" I shout, throwing my hands in the air. "Go home."

"You heard her," Ember says calmly from her position next to a man wearing an SKMC cut. "You need to leave."

Blue eyes, so like my own, bore down on me. "Where is he?"

"Who?"

"Screamer," Shuffle clarifies and shifts to look at the biker next to Ember. "Get his fucking ass out here."

"I don't answer to you," the man says.

Shuffle lunges at him, and all hell breaks loose. Fists fly, bodies crash to the floor, and blood spurts from wounds. It all happens so fast that I barely have time to step away from the fray.

As I'm backing up, I hit something solid. I whip around and see Screamer. He's flushed with rage and coiled tighter than a rattler ready to strike.

"Go to my room," he orders just before diving into the mix.

CHAPTER 20
SCREAMER

It's time to put my game face on.

Pain radiates through my jaw, and my knuckles are raw, but I ignore it. When I heard the commotion from church, my blood ran cold as I raced into the common area. Then I saw the fighting, and Roxie standing there so close to the mayhem, and I broke.

"Screamer, stop!"

Her pleas penetrate the haze in my mind, and my fist freezes mid-air. Unfortunately, Shuffle takes that opportunity to land a solid blow to my face. My skin splits open on my cheek, and he throws another punch.

"Shuffle!" Roxie screams.

Her brother and I roll around on the floor, trading jabs. We're so caught up in pummeling each other that Roxie's nearness doesn't register. And when she grabs the back of her brother's shirt to try and pull him off me, he doesn't realize it's her until it's too late.

Shuffle throws his head back to dislodge her, catching her in the chest. She stumbles backward, falling to her ass on the floor and hitting her head.

"Ouch," she shrieks.

I immediately shove Shuffle away from me and scramble to her side. "Jesus, are you okay?"

Her eyes seem unfocused, but she manages to nod. "I'm—"

"Get away from her!" Shuffle demands, and I jump to my feet and whirl on him.

My chest heaves, and my fists clench. "I'm gonna fucking kill you for hurting her," I snarl.

"Fuck you," he barks. "I told you that she's off-limits."

He reaches for my cut, but Roxie slides between us. I hadn't even realized she got up.

"Both of you, stop!" She pushes on my chest, and I take a step back. She does the same to her brother, but he's not as cooperative. "Ryan, stop."

"I've got a dead brother on the side of the road," Shuffle begins. "And you're here with him. Jesus, Rox, you were engaged to be married not that long ago. What the hell is wrong with you?"

I growl, intent on setting him straight, but Roxie beats me to the punch.

"What's wrong with me?" she snaps. "God, Ryan, you're such an asshole. You're right… Saint is dead. And yes, I came here. But I did it for you!"

He rears back as if slapped. "Whaddya mean you did it for me?"

"Maybe you two should take this somewhere more private," Crow suggests, and that's when I notice that the rest of the fighting has ceased, and all eyes are on me, Roxie, and Shuffle.

"No, that's okay," Roxie states. "If he wants answers, he's gonna get answers." She keeps her gaze level on her brother. "You want to know the truth, Ry? Will that make you happy?"

"Dammit, Rox, spit it out," he commands.

She wraps her arms around herself and starts to pace. Shuffle follows her every move, and when she doesn't 'spit it out', he takes a step toward her. I grab his shirt to stop him.

"Give her a minute," I bite out.

"She's my sister," Shuffle argues. "I'll—"

"Saint is dead because of me," she blurts, and his head whips in her direction.

"What?"

Roxie takes a deep breath and moves to stand in front of her brother. She squares her shoulders and rubs the back of her head. "You heard me. He's dead because of me. I…" She licks her lips. "Jace didn't break up with me. I left him because he beat the shit out of me."

That seems to knock the wind from Shuffle's sails, and his shoulders sag. Over the next few minutes, she spills all the sordid details of her relationship with Jace, how he hurt her, and how she ran. By the time she finishes, she's crying, and I'm doing everything in my power not to lift her into my arms and carry her to my room to console her.

"So, you think Jace killed Saint?" Shuffle asks.

Crow steps forward and hands him the note we found with Saint. "Here."

Shuffle reads it and swears under his breath. "Where can we find him?"

"That's just it," I say. "We have no clue. I filled Addison in, and she's got her people working on it. I'm guessing the police are already at the scene."

Shuffle nods. "Okay. Yeah, that's good."

Normally, we don't like to involve law enforcement. But Addison is one of the good ones, and we all trust her. The fact that Shuffle isn't fighting her involvement tells me all I need to know: He might be pissed at me, but he trusts us enough to follow suit with Addison.

"Ry, please believe me," Roxie cries. "The only

reason I didn't call you or come to you is because I don't know what more Jace will do. Saint's gone. I can't lose you, too."

"I believe you," he assures her. "But him?" Shuffle nods in my direction. "You hate bikers."

"I don't hate bikers," she insists.

Her brother moves to stand toe to toe with me. "I warned you to stay away from her, Screamer."

"You did."

"If I remember correctly, I also told you I'd gut the next guy who hurt her."

I look from him to Roxie. "Have I hurt you, sweetheart?" She shakes her head, and I return my attention to him. "See. No reason to spill guts."

"What part of off-limits don't you understand?" he counters.

"You don't get to—"

"She's. Mine," I tell him, cutting Roxie off.

"I don't belong to you," she argues.

"Are you claiming her?" Shuffle asks.

"Jesus, I'm standing right here." Roxie waves her hands.

"I am," I confirm, ignoring her.

"No, he's not," she snaps.

"Yes, sweetheart," I say without looking at her. "I am. It doesn't change anything other than your brother can't do shit about you being here."

"He couldn't before," she insists.

"Well," Crow chimes in, coming to stand next to me. "Now that that's settled, I think we all need to talk about the situation with Roxie's ex."

"Nothing is settled," Roxie gripes.

Shuffle opens his mouth to argue, but Addison comes running into the common area with her cell up to her ear.

"Hey, sorry to interrupt, but I've got one of my detectives on the phone," she says. "They want to know if you want them to notify Rae about Saint, or if you'd prefer to do it."

"That's an option?" Shuffle asks.

"Of course," Addison says matter-of-factly. "I know how clubs work. And I also know that it will probably be easier for her to hear the news from someone she knows."

"I'll tell her," Roxie says.

"Are you sure?" I ask, worried about how that conversation will affect her.

Roxie nods. "Yeah."

"Do you want me to go with you?" Addison asks.

Roxie seems to think about it for a minute before replaying. "That'd be great, thanks."

Addison walks away to relay the message to her detective, and Crow and Shuffle face each other again.

"How 'bout we head into our meeting room?" Crow asks. "We can discuss how to proceed with your sister's ex."

Shuffle looks to his VP, Bear, who nods. "Yeah, okay."

My brothers, and the LTMC members move through the common area toward the meeting room. I remain behind to talk to Roxie for a minute.

"Are you sure you'll be okay talking to Rae?" I ask again.

"No," she whispers. "But it's not about me, is it?"

Heaving a sigh, I lean in and kiss her forehead. "Come back here after?"

"Okay."

"Call me if you need me."

"I will."

With that, she walks out of the clubhouse. A few minutes later, Addison joins her, and I hear Addison's car start.

Heart cracked, and body aching, I trudge to the meeting room. It's time to put my game face on.

CHAPTER 21
ROXIE

MAKE ME FEEL SOMETHING GOOD.

"Fuck, that was rough."

I stare out the passenger window of Addison's vehicle. We just left Rae at the LTMC clubhouse with her mom and sister. When I told her about Saint, she broke down, begging me to tell her I was lying. Of course, I couldn't do that. What I could do was hold her while she cried, so I did. My borrowed hoodie is wet, and my heart is in pieces.

"Yeah," I agree quietly.

Addison reaches across the console and squeezes my hand. "She'll be okay, Roxie. It's going to be hard, and she'll have days where living seems impossible, but with time, she'll start to move forward and heal."

I scoff. "Is that what you would do if Crow died?"

"Honestly? I don't know. A life without him... It's unimaginable."

"Exactly."

Silence surrounds us for a few minutes, and I think about Saint and Rae. Shit, they were so in love. He'd happily have given his life for her, but to give it because of me... It's not right.

"So," Addison says, pulling me out of my thoughts. "You and Screamer, huh?"

"There is no me and Screamer," I say.

"Keep telling yourself that."

"We don't even know each other."

"Let me ask you a question." She pauses, taking a deep breath. "How would you feel if that had been Screamer and not Saint?"

I contemplate how to answer that. The truth is, I don't know. An image of Screamer lying on the road with lifeless eyes flashes in my mind, and I shudder.

You do know.

All of my arguments about us barely knowing each other, all of my fear and doubt and trust issues melt away. I'd be devastated if Screamer died. How I got to this point, I don't have a fucking clue. Maybe it started when he told me about Ally. Or maybe it was when he asked me who broke my ribs because at that moment, I knew he cared enough to look beyond the surface, despite having just met me.

"Roxie?" Addison prods.

"Sad," I say. "I'd be sad."

The rest of the drive passes by in a blur. When we reach the clubhouse, I spot my brother's bike, as well as Bear's. The rest of LTMC seems to have left.

Addison and I walk inside, and I immediately scan the room for Screamer. Relief washes over me when I spot him at the bar with Crow and my brother. As if linked by an invisible tether, he turns, and his eyes land on me.

He sets down his beer and closes the distance between us.

"You okay?" he asks.

"I'll leave you two alone," Addison says before I can answer, and she crosses the room to Crow.

"Answer me, sweetheart. Are you okay?"

I burst into tears, shaking my head. "No."

Before I know what's happening, Screamer scoops me into his arms and carries me to his room. He kicks the door shut behind him and sets me on the bed. Then he straightens and stares down at me.

"Fuck, you're beautiful. Even when you're crying." The sound that passes my lips at his assessment is a cross between a snort and a laugh. "Tell me what to do," he pleads.

I rub my eyes, and my breath hitches. "Hold me?"

He doesn't hesitate. Lifting me with one arm, he yanks his comforter back with the other, and then he sets me back down and slides in next to me. I curl into his side, and he wraps me in his embrace.

"How's Rae?" he asks after several minutes.

"Broken."

"Understandable."

I nod and push myself back so I can look him in the eye. "I don't know how she's going to get through this."

"She will. She's got a lot of people looking out for her."

"I know."

"What about you? Will you get through it?"

"I…" I clear my throat. "Will you help me?"

"I'll do anything," he says, his voice barely above a whisper.

"Anything?"

"Anything," he confirms.

I slide my hands under his shirt and up his chest. Screamer tenses, and his skin ripples under my touch.

"Make me feel something good."

He grabs my hands to stop my movements. "Are you sure about this, Roxie? Because once we cross that bridge, there's no going back."

Am I sure? No. Am I going to do it anyway? Hell, yes.

"I'm sure."

Screamer climbs out of the bed, pulling me to my feet with him. His heated gaze travels the length of my body, from my head to my toes and back again. "You look fucking incredible in my clothes."

Heat creeps into my cheeks, but there's no time for embarrassment. Screamer grabs the hem of the hoodie and tugs it over my head. Next, he pushes the sweatpants over my hips, exposing my green lace thong.

"Goddamn, you're beautiful," he breathes. "Every inch of you is perfection."

Dropping to his knees, he tucks his thumbs into the waistband of my panties and slides them down my legs to pool at my feet. Then he's on me, feasting on my clit and pussy like a starving man.

My legs shake, so he urges me back until I hit the bed. I fall to my ass, and he grabs my ankles to dangle my limbs over his shoulders. All the while, he doesn't stop flicking his tongue over my clit.

"Ah, fuck," I moan.

"That's it, sweetheart." He brings his hand up and shoves a finger inside my cunt, then another. "Come for me," he orders, and my orgasm crashes over me like a breaking wave in the ocean.

As my body begins to calm, Screamer stands and begins to strip. My eyes are heavy, hooded, and saliva fills my mouth at the sight of him. The tattoo on his chest catches my attention, and I reach out to trace my fingers over it.

"Python's work," he tells me. "Got it after Ally and my parents were killed."

"It's beautiful."

"It is," he agrees as he pushes me to my back and climbs on top of me to straddle my hips. "But I don't want to talk about that."

I lock eyes with him. "Me either."

Screamer dips his head to capture a nipple between his teeth. He nips then licks to soothe the sting. He repeats this several times before he trails kisses up my chest and over my chin.

I cup his cheeks and pull him to my mouth, kissing him with feral need. Thinking becomes impossible, which is exactly what I want.

Breaking apart to catch my breath, I move my lips to his ear. "Fuck me, Screamer," I whisper.

He reaches between us and grabs his hard length to line up with my entrance. My pussy is soaked, and when he pushes inside, I swear it weeps with joy. He wasn't kidding about his eight inches.

"You take me so well, Roxie," he pants.

We find a rhythm, and with every one of his thrusts, I lift my hips to meet his. My body stretches to accommodate his length and girth, and the way he fills me feels exquisite.

"Make me come, Ben," I beg. "Please make me come again."

"Say that again."

"Ben," I say, knowing exactly what he wants to hear. "Fuck, Ben."

He slides his hand down my stomach and presses his thumb against my clit to rub hard and fast circles. My breathing is ragged, my flesh is slick with sweat, and I'm loving every second.

"Come on, sweetheart," he groans. "Come with me."

His cock swells, and his movements become jerky. We shatter, clinging to one another as if our lives depend on it. The orgasm seems to go on forever, but eventually, Screamer rolls to the side, sliding out of my slick heat, and pulls me into his side.

"Feel better?" he finally asks after he catches his breath.

His question brings the events of the day to the forefront of my mind. "Physically, yes. Emotionally, no."

"Fair."

Unable to stop it, I yawn, stretching my body as I do. "I'm so damn tired."

He kisses the top of my head. "Get some sleep."

"You'll be here when I wake up?"

"Promise, sweetheart."

CHAPTER 22
SCREAMER

Wrong.

"Our guy couldn't find him."

Drumming my fingers on the table, I can't stop thinking about the woman still in my bed. I kept my promise and was there when she woke up... the first time. After we fucked again, she fell back to sleep, and I came to church. Shuffle and a few of his brothers are present, and it's disconcerting to know his sister is naked under the same roof.

"Addison and her detectives haven't either," Crow states.

"What about you?" I ask, turning my attention to Tracer. "Find anything?"

He stares at me for a long moment, and I give him an almost imperceptible nod. He approached me before church was called to order and asked if I was okay with him sharing the fact that I asked him to dig into Roxie. I told him to go ahead, that I have nothing to hide anymore because Roxie's safety takes priority over my secrets.

"Well, per your request," he begins. "I dug into Roxie, which led me to Jace."

"You were snooping on my sister?" Shuffle snarls.

"Don't," Crow barks. "I get that you're pissed about her being with Screamer, but it is what it is. Let it go."

Shuffle settles into his chair. "Fine. But know that I'm only giving in because this is your house, not mine."

"Understood." Crow looks to Tracer. "Continue."

"Honestly, there wasn't much to find on Roxie. No criminal record, no dirty laundry, so to speak."

"You thought you'd find otherwise?" Shuffle asks.

"No," Tracer admits. "But I did come across her social media accounts, and that's where things get juicy."

"How so?" I demand.

"Well, her relationship is documented in her posts and pictures. Seems they were happy together. Now, we all know that was a front, at least toward the end. But you'd never guess it."

"Okay, but do you have anything we don't know?" Journey asks.

"I'm getting to that. So, Roxie used to post every day, some days more than once. Then her posts just stopped. I'm assuming that's when she left Jace and came here."

"Makes sense," Python says. "She was running from him, and social media makes it too easy to be tracked."

"Right. I thought the same thing," Tracer explains. "The weird thing is, Jace never commented on anything until *after* she left. And the comments were weird. He'd go from gushing over how pretty she looks in a picture to calling her a whore for wishing a male friend 'happy birthday'."

"So, he's crazy," Jackyl, our club doc, states.

"Pretty much," Tracer confirms. "The only social media activity he has is those comments on Roxie's profile. He also doesn't have a criminal record. On paper, he's a stand-up guy."

"Tell that to Rae," Shuffle bites out.

Tracer raises his hands. "Just giving facts, man."

"I'm not buying that he's squeaky clean," Poker chimes in. "There's no way that beating Roxie is the first wrong thing he's ever done."

"Agreed," I add. "He's just managed to not get caught."

"Which makes this even harder because it means he's smart," Crow says.

"I have an idea," Bear says from where he's standing against the wall, and all eyes turn to him.

"What's that?" Crow and Shuffle ask simultaneously.

"Rather than waste another minute on this prick, we should vote on what essentially would amount to a bounty on his head."

"Explain," Shuffle demands.

"I mean, if this guy is so hard to track down, then we have to assume that's not going to change. I propose that Roxie be put under twenty-four-seven guard, and the rest of us keep our eyes and ears open. If we come across the bastard, take him out. It's clean and simple. And it doesn't alert him in any way if he's watching us."

"Roxie will never go for being under guard," I say, knowing it'll piss her the fuck off.

Shuffle smirks. "What she doesn't know won't hurt her."

"You want me to lie to her?" I counter. "After everything she's been through, that's not happening."

Her brother sighs. "Fine. Tell her, but explain that it's temporary. Shit, it can be you who's with her at all times. At this point, I don't give a damn as long as she's safe."

"You're trusting me with her?"

"You claimed her, didn't you?"

"I did."

"Then, yeah, I'm trusting you. If there's one thing I know for sure, it's that when a biker claims a woman, they will do whatever the fuck it takes to protect her."

"Damn straight," I agree.

"All in favor of Bear's plan, thump twice," Crow orders.

Every man in the room pounds the table or wall two times.

"Good. Now, Addison is going to continue to investigate Saint's death. She knows how the club works, so when Jace turns up dead, there'll be no heat from police."

"You sure about that?" Creep asks, speaking for the first time since church started.

"I'd stake my life on it."

Creep nods.

"In the meantime," Journey begins. "Is there anything we can do to help with Saint's funeral?"

"At the moment, no," Shuffle responds. "If that changes, I'll let you know."

"Please do," Crow says.

Church is called to an end, and each man funnels out of the room. Each man but Shuffle and me.

"She slept in your bed last night, didn't she?" he asks me, his eyes narrow.

"Do you really want me to answer that?"

He hesitates for a brief moment before shaking his head. "No. Know this, Screamer. I meant what I said about gutting you if you hurt her."

"I know."

"Then I wish you luck."

"What?"

He chuckles darkly. "You're the one who's going to tell her about her new situation with having a guard. She's not going to like that."

He walks away from me, and I swear I hear him whistling gleefully as he does. I inhale deeply and mentally prepare myself for the conversation I have to have. She might be mad at first, but she'll understand.

Right?

Wrong.

Roxie was definitely angry and did *not* understand.

CHAPTER 23
ROXIE

Never gonna happen.

Two months later...

"I'm fine."

Rae's shout reaches me from across the room and over the music. I glance in her direction and see her trying to pull her empty glass from Mark's hands. He's running the bar tonight, and Rae is, well, doing the same thing she's been doing since Saint's funeral… getting wasted.

I don't blame her. Saint was her entire world. She lived and breathed for him, and he for her. I can't imagine what she's going through. Fuck, Screamer and I have only been together for a month, sort of, and losing him would break me in ways that shouldn't be possible. Rae and Saint had *years*.

"Hey, Rae," I say when I reach her side. "Why don't we go sit down?"

She slaps my hands away. "I don't wanna sit. I wanna drink."

Which is why I'm here. Shuffle asked me to return to the LTMC clubhouse to help with her because none of them knew what to do. The truth is, there's nothing anyone can do but listen and be there when she crashes. Because she *will* crash.

There will come a day when Rae wakes up sober, and her loss will shatter her all over again. For now, though, she's content to drink her pain away, and I'm content to let her… to a degree.

"I know you do," I say gently. "I'm not asking you to stop drinking."

"Oh." She pouts. "Tell him that then," she said, pointing at Mark.

"Mark, get her another drink, please," I order, then silently mouth, "Water."

Rae is so far gone that she won't notice the difference. Impossible to comprehend that level of intoxication, but trust me. She's found it.

"You got it, Rox."

He fills a glass with water and ice before handing it to me.

"C'mon, Rae," I urge, leading her to the couch.

She tries to veer toward the juke box, but I hold her steady. "I'll find something to play, okay?"

"'Kay."

Rae flops onto the sofa, leaning her head against the back. Her eyes close, and it's only minutes before she's softly snoring. I take the glass of water from her hand before it spills and carry it back to the bar.

"I hate seeing her like this," Mark comments.

"You and me both."

"Is there anything I can do? Other than serving her copious amounts of booze?"

I smile sadly and shake my head. "No. She'll work her way through this in her own way and her own time."

"Okay." He dumps the water in the sink. "Can I get you anything to drink?"

"Nah, I'm good. I've gotta work in the morning."

"How's the new job going?"

A month after Screamer informed me that I'd be under lock and key, I told him that I was going job hunting. At first, he argued, but I reminded him that Jace hadn't done anything since Saint, and through conversations with Sammie, Melody, and Greg, we were able to confirm that he was back at the home he and I shared and had been seen out with several different women.

The Soulless Kings' and Limitless Throttle MCs had reconvened and agreed that, while Jace was still out there, the threat he posed was considerably less with him in a different state.

"It's great," I reply, grinning.

I started working at a local domestic violence shelter as a peer counselor and am taking night classes for a degree in psychology. This isn't the path I thought I'd be on, but life had other plans. I love the new plan, though.

"Good, I'm glad."

"Hey, um, I've been meaning to ask you," I begin. "Have you talked to Seth lately?"

The night Saint beat the shit out of him, Seth had been banned from the club. He'd only been a prospect, so that's the worst punishment he received.

Mark shakes his head. "Nope. Figured no good could come from talking to him. I love Limitless Throttle and really want to earn my patch. That won't happen if I interact with someone banned."

"True enough," I agree.

Mark reaches across the bar and rests his hand on top of mine. There's no spark, no hint of anything beyond the friendship we've developed.

"I really am sorry about that night, Rox," he says solemnly.

I smile. "You've apologized a million times. It's fine, Mark. Really. Let it go because I have."

He releases a pent-up breath. "Thanks."

"Get your hands off my woman."

I whirl around to see Screamer striding toward me. He and I come and go from each clubhouse as we please, and it's nice seeing him so comfortable in both locations.

"Leave him alone," I chide even as Mark pulls his hand away.

"Didn't mean any disrespect," Mark says.

Screamer laughs. "It's fine, kid. I was just yanking your dick."

Mark cups his crotch. "Yeah, no," he says, scrunching his nose.

"You know what I mean."

"I do. Still… no."

"Fine, don't take a joke." Screamer practically dismisses Mark and settles his mouth over mine for a toe-curling kiss. "How was your day, sweetheart?"

"It was good," I tell him. "I was able to secure housing for that mother and her three kids in another state. Linda is driving them to the new location tomorrow, which means that bastard husband of hers won't be able to find her again."

"That's great."

"It really is." I glance across the room at Rae. "She's passed out again."

Screamer follows my line of sight and sighs. "Yo, Mark," he says without looking at the prospect. "Mind carrying her to her room?"

"No problem."

Suddenly, I'm lifted off my feet and slung over Screamer's shoulder. "And I'm gonna carry you to your room, sweetheart."

I laugh and hit him in the back, pretending to put up a fight. He only swats my ass, sending a delicious tingle to spread to my pussy. Entering my room, he kicks the door shut and tosses me on the bed.

"I'm gonna ravish you," he taunts, and I watch greedily as he takes his clothes off.

"I'm all for it," I admit. "But first, I wanted to talk to you about something."

He groans. "Can it wait?" Cock in his hand, he gives it a few sharp tugs.

I shake my head. There was a time, right after Jace, I wouldn't have stood my ground, but I know with Screamer, I can, and he won't be mad.

"Okay." He lets go of his dick and crawls onto the mattress to sit beside me. "What's up?"

"Things have been good lately, right? Like, really good?"

He brushes a strand of hair behind my ear. "Absolutely."

"And we're pretty sure Jace is no longer an issue since we know he's not in Texas."

"Pretty sure, yes, but not a hundred percent."

I wave a hand dismissively. "As long as he's breathing, we'll never be a hundred percent. But I can't live my life in fear forever."

"No, you can't."

"So, I've been thinking…"

"Uh-oh," he teases.

I slap him playfully, rolling my eyes. "I wanna invite Greg, Sammie, and Melody for a visit."

Screamer seems to ponder a moment before nodding. "Go for it."

"Really?"

"Sweetheart, they're your friends. I'm good with whatever you want to do." He pauses and frowns. "Unless you tell me you wanna go back to Jace. Then we'd have a problem."

"Never gonna happen."

"I know. But yeah, give 'em a call and plan something. We can host them at my clubhouse. There's plenty of space. I know you guys are short on rooms here now that Rae's moved in."

The reminder of Rae douses some of my good mood, but I refuse to let it completely ruin my happiness. I love Rae and am here for her, but not at the expense of myself.

"I'll give 'em a call in the morning." I thread my fingers through his hair and pull his head down, so my lips are inches from his. "But first, I believe you had something different in mind when you carried me in here."

CHAPTER 24
SCREAMER

Doesn't hurt to be prepared.

"Want me to come with?"

I slow my steps to respond to Poker. It's been a week since Roxie invited her friends for a visit, and since they decided to make a road trip out of it, we don't have an exact time for their arrival, which means I'm running around like a chicken with its head cut off to get ready.

"Nah, I'm good," I tell him.

"Anything I can do here?"

I glance around to survey the clubhouse. "Maybe double-check that the spare rooms are ready."

"Already done. Meri made sure before she left for her shift at the bar."

"Awesome. Thanks."

"No problem."

Before he can slow me down further, I make my way outside and climb into my truck. I'd much rather ride my Harley, but kegs don't fit on a bike. I'm almost to town when my cell rings. I answer it via the connected Bluetooth.

"Hey, sweetheart."

"How'd you know it was me?" Roxie asks sweetly.

"Because it's noon, which means you're on your lunch break."

"Right."

"How's your day going?"

"Good. I just got a text from Greg saying their ETA is five-thirty."

"Damn, they're making good time."

"Sammie's driving. She's got a lead foot."

I chuckle. "Well, I can't wait to meet them."

A shuffling noise comes through the line, and I wait while Roxie speaks to someone.

"I gotta go," she says when she's done. "I've got a walk-in."

"Okay. Just make sure you eat at some point."

"I will. Love you."

She disconnects the call, giving me no chance to respond.

Did she just say what I think she said?

We haven't said those words to each other yet. I debate on calling her back but decide against it. She's at work. She probably said it out of reflex.

Yeah. Yeah, that's it.

And if that isn't it? I'd be the happiest I've ever been. I love her, too. I've chosen not to say it to her because I don't want her to feel pressured. I promised her that I'm a patient man, and that we could take our relationship at her pace, and I won't break that promise.

The rest of the way into town, I'm on cloud nine. I park downtown and go into the liquor store to pick up the kegs I ordered. Once those are loaded into the back of the truck, I walk to one of the shops down the street. I'm not a flashy man, and I'm unapologetically simple. That being said, tonight is special to Roxie, so I'm going to put in a little extra effort.

I purchase a new pair of jeans and a long-sleeved Henley. Satisfied that she'll appreciate the small gesture, I make my way back to the truck. I'm sidetracked, though, when I spot the jeweler across the street. Diamonds sparkle in the display windows, and I find myself crossing the road and entering the store.

"Hello," a woman greets. "How can I help you today?"

Feeling like a bull in a china shop, I glance around. "Not sure you can, really," I admit. "Wasn't planning on coming in here."

"Well, feel free to look around, and if you find yourself needing assistance, let me know."

"Thanks."

I browse the cases of rings for what feels like hours, although it's probably more like thirty minutes. The woman checks on me a few times but otherwise leaves me alone to contemplate what the fuck I'm doing.

I don't even know if Roxie meant it when she said, 'love you'. Shit, we've only been together for a few months. The problem with all of that is it doesn't seem to matter one single iota.

I do love her. The more time I spend with her, the more I can't fathom life without her. I claimed her before she was ready, so I won't propose to her yet. Doesn't hurt to be prepared, though.

Right?

"Can I see that one, please?" I ask, pointing to a ring that has a solitaire diamond nestled among a circle of black diamonds.

"Of course."

When I return to the clubhouse, it's with three kegs, a new outfit, and a very expensive engagement ring. Poker helps me carry in the beer, and as soon as it's unloaded, I make a beeline for my room.

I tuck the black velvet ring box into a drawer and head to the shower.

"Love you, too, sweetheart," I whisper to the empty room.

CHAPTER 25
ROXIE

Help.

"Shouldn't you be going?"

I lift my head and set my pen on top of the stack of files I was going through. Linda leans her shoulder against the door jam, and she looks tired. It's been a long day with two new intakes.

"I will in a minute," I tell her. "Just wanna finish this up first."

"Don't stay too long. I know you've got big plans tonight."

I smile at the reminder. "I do. But I got a text an hour ago that they got caught in standstill traffic due to an accident."

"That sucks."

"Tell me about it. I wish they would've flown.

Their journey would've been more predictable. Anyway, I'll be out of here in ten. Promise."

"Okay. I'm gonna head out if you're good to lock up. I've already checked on the shelter residents, and the evening staff are over on that side of the building. All you have to do is take care of the office area."

"Got it. Have a good night."

"You, too. And think of me when you're having fun."

I laugh at her expression. "Nothing planned with the kids tonight?"

"Yeah. We're going out to dinner at Red Lobster for the middle one's birthday."

"That sounds like fun."

"Roxie, I've got four kids and a husband who might as well be my fifth. Nothing about going out to dinner is fun."

"Uh-huh. Keep telling yourself that."

With that, she leaves for the evening. I know she loves her family and spending time with them. But I make a mental note to invite her out for a drink sometime. It certainly couldn't hurt for her to spend time with friends and remember that she's more than a wife and mother.

I lock the door twenty minutes later and cross the street to the parking garage where my Harley awaits me. As I'm walking, I send a quick text to Screamer, letting him know that I'm running a little late but am on my way. Then I shove it into my pocket.

I'm two miles down the road when my cell vibrates against my side with an incoming call. I forgot to put my earbud in, so I ignore it, sure that it's Screamer. When the phone rings again, and then again for a third and fourth time, I pull over and lower the kickstand.

Glancing at the screen, I frown. Melody's number flashes on the screen and calling back-to-back like she is worries me.

"Hey, girl. Please tell me y'all aren't stuck in traffic again," I say when I answer.

"Roxanne."

My heart skips a beat at the sound of Jace's voice. "Where the fuck is Melody?" I demand. If he's got her phone, he's got her. He's also likely got the others. "Greg and Sammie? Let me talk to them."

"I don't think so," he says.

"What do you want?" I ask, fear stealing my breath.

"It's quite simple, Roxanne. I want…" He inhales deeply before sighing in a way that has me wondering if he's masturbating. "You."

"That's not gonna happen."

"Oh, but it will. You see, if I don't get you, I'll kill your friends. Then I'll go straight to Marble Falls and kill your boyfriend. Or should I say boy*friends*? Oh, wait. I already killed the one. I forgot."

At the reminder of Saint, I wince. Addison, the police, and the clubs haven't been able to tie the accident to Jace. Other than the note he left, there wasn't enough evidence for the District Attorney to issue an arrest warrant.

"Fine," I say through clenched teeth. "Where are you?"

He rattles off a location. "You've got thirty minutes before I start killing. Oh, and this should go without saying, but don't call anyone. It won't end well for you or them if you do."

With that, he disconnects the call, and I sit for a moment, trying hard to suck air into my lungs. I know I can't risk calling Screamer, not yet anyway. I've gotta get closer to Jace before I alert anyone. For all I know, Jace is monitoring my phone, and if that's the case, I'm not going to tip him off too early that I've got people coming to my rescue.

I put the coordinates he rattled off into my GPS and see that it's the middle of nowhere. Taking off down the road, I silently pray that my friends can hold on until I get there.

Twenty-seven minutes later, I come to a stop when I reach what appears to be an abandoned vehicle. The road is surrounded by woods on both sides, and the blinking dot on my map shows me that Jace has Greg, Melody, and Sammie deep among the trees.

I hop off my bike and rush to the car, peering in the windows. There's no sign that indicates this is the rental my friends had, so I assume it's Jace's.

Where the fuck is their car? Where'd he get them?

I take my cell out of my pocket and pull up my texts to send one to Screamer.

> Me: Help, Jace, 911

Dropping my phone to the ground so Jace can't see that I sent the text if he isn't monitoring it and searches me, I take off at a run.

"Jace!" I yell, hoping he hears me since my thirty minutes are up. "I'm here!"

CHAPTER 26
SCREAMER

THAT'S RIGHT, SWEETHEART. I'M NOT HIM.

"Dude, where's your girl?"

Frowning, I glance at the clock on the wall. It's six-fifteen, and Roxie should've been home almost an hour ago. I'm not super worried because sometimes the shelter gets an intake late in the day or after hours. Domestic violence doesn't stick to a nine to five workday.

"She'll be here soon, I'm sure."

I reach into my back pocket for my cell but come up empty. Realizing I must have left it in my room in my other pair of jeans, I go get it. When I spot it on the floor, I pick it up and grin when I see I've got two missed texts from Roxie. I don't have the text previews enabled on my phone so when I open the messaging app and read them, my knees threaten to buckle.

> Roxie: Running a little late but on my way
>
> Roxie: Help, Jace, 911

Sprinting into action, I run out of my room and find Tracer in the common area.

"Please tell me you can track Roxie's phone," I demand, grabbing him by the shoulders.

"Of course," he replies. "What's wrong?"

I race to the door. "Text me her location!"

Without telling anyone what's going on, I fire up my Harley, shove my Bluetooth earbud in, and tear out of the gravel lot. Her last text to me came through about a half hour ago, and that scares the shit out of me.

"What?" I snap, answering a call that comes through a few minutes later.

"What's going on?" Crow demands, and I can barely hear him over the roar of my engine.

"Jace has Roxie."

"Son of a bitch," he bites out. "Shuffle and I will be right behind you."

"Tracer's got the location," I tell him. "And Crow?"

"Yeah?"

"Bring Jackyl. She might need medical attention."

Disconnecting the call, I rev the throttle. A text comes through, and I have Siri read it to me, so I don't get distracted and end up like Saint.

"From Tracer. North of town, approximately nineteen miles, heavily wooded area, phone is stationary."

I try to picture the area he's talking about and groan when I realize that it's the perfect place to take a prisoner. The woods are on state land, and there are no trespassing signs posted all over the place. Barely any traffic uses those roads which means Jace can do whatever he wants to Roxie without fear of being found.

What should've taken me forty minutes takes me only twenty-five, and they're the longest twenty-five minutes of my life. I spot Roxie's Harley first and then the abandoned vehicle. Without bothering with my kickstand, I hop off my bike and let it fall to the ground.

I love my bike, but at the end of the day, it's just a hunk of metal.

"Roxie!" I shout, shoving my way through the trees and ignoring the way branches tear through my shirt and skin. "Roxie!"

C'mon, sweetheart. Give me some sort of clue as to where you are.

"Roxanne is occupied at the moment!" a male voice echoes through the air.

That'll do.

I slow my pace to yank my gun out of my ankle holster, grateful that I wear it at all times. After ensuring the safety is off, I run as fast as I can in the direction I think the voice came from. Seconds later, I hear the same man talking shit to someone.

Skidding to a stop when I see Roxie, I scan the area. Jace is standing next to the tree that Roxie is tied to, and he's holding a whip that appears to be dripping blood from the tip. The sun is starting to set, and with the forest surroundings, it's hard to see.

Roxie is naked, and slash marks crisscross her torso. Her head hangs limply to the side, and there's something covering her mouth. There are also three others tied to different trees and either unconscious or dead, and I can only assume they're the friends who were coming for a visit.

"Jesus," I whisper harshly.

"I knew she couldn't resist calling you," Jace says calmly. "Which is why I started the party early."

"You're a sick fuck, you know that?"

He drags the whip through the dirt. "I'm okay with that. Wanna know why?"

"Why?"

"Because sick fuck or not, I'm the one who will be walking away from here with Roxanne on my arm."

If she can even walk.

I lift my gun and aim it at his head. My brain screams at me to pull the trigger, but I don't. Not yet. I need answers first. Roxie is going to have questions, and I'll be damned if I take away her chance to know whatever it is that will make her feel better when this is all over.

"Roxie, sweetheart," I call to her. "C'mon, Rox, wake up for me."

She tries to lift her head and moans.

"Her name is Roxanne," Jace seethes.

"Why are you doing this?" I ask.

"She agreed to be my wife, and that's what she's going to be," he says as if I should've known the answer.

"And then you beat her," I remind him. "She left you, Jace. She doesn't love you."

"You think I give a shit about love?" he snaps. "It took me two years to make Roxanne marriage material. I had her right where I wanted her."

"She's not an animal," I growl. "She's a fucking human, and she deserves so much more than you."

"Like what? You?"

"Honestly, it doesn't even matter if it's me or

some other man, as long as it's not you, as long as she's happy."

As soon as the words leave my mouth, I realize how true they are. Losing Roxie would probably kill me, but the most important thing is that she's happy. If she's alive and not with Jace, I can live with that.

"Mmmm," she moans, forcing my gaze to waver from Jace. "S-Screamer?"

"I'm here, sweetheart," I say.

She lifts her head at an agonizingly slow pace and locks her eyes on mine. "Kill him."

Without missing a beat, I squeeze the trigger. The bullet goes through Jace's chest, and I'm at Roxie's side before his body even hits the ground.

"Fuck, sweetheart, I'm so sorry," I whisper as I work the ropes wound around her body and the tree trunk.

"F-for what?"

"For letting him get to you. I should've known you weren't safe. I should've kept you gua—"

"Screamer," she whispers.

"Yeah?"

"Shut up."

The second she's free, I cradle her in my arms and lower her to the ground. I take my cut off and peel my shirt over my head to cover her. She's shivering, her teeth audibly chattering in the quiet night.

"I'm gonna get your friends down, okay?"

She nods. "He knocked them out after…" Roxie spits blood from her mouth before continuing. "After he made them watch him whip me. Said he needed to make them pay for helping me leave."

Relief courses through me that they're alive. Roxie still blames herself for Saint. There's no telling what she'd do if she thought these three were dead because of her.

As I untie the ropes holding them each up, the sound of leaves crunching filters into the silence. Seconds later, Crow, Shuffle, Journey, Bear, and Jackyl burst through the trees, guns drawn.

"You're a little late," I drawl. "Jackyl, go check on Roxie. The rest of you, help me get them down."

Shuffle follows Jackyl to his sister's side. As soon as Greg, Melody, and Sammie are free and lying on the ground, I return to Roxie.

"She's gonna be okay," Jackyl says, assessing her wounds. "There'll be scars, both inside and out, I'm afraid, but I'll get an IV with fluids, antibiotics, and pain meds started as soon as we get her back to the clubhouse. That'll help a lot."

"She's coming home with me," Shuffle states flatly.

"No, I'm not," Roxie says, hissing through her

teeth as she tries to sit up. "I'm going with Screamer."

Shuffle looks like he wants to argue, but he wisely keeps any protests to himself.

"I'll take care of her, man," I assure him.

He nods and straightens to his full height. "You can't keep her away from me."

"Wouldn't dream of it. You're her brother."

Is that what Shuffle's been worried about, that because we're in different clubs I won't let Roxie spend time with him? No wonder he's been a pain in the ass.

"Jace said the same thing."

"I'm no—"

"He's not Jace," Roxie barks with more force than she should be capable of at the moment.

I cup her cheeks. "That's right, sweetheart. I'm not him."

It takes a while to get everyone back to the vehicles, and as I carry Roxie through the trees, a thought occurs to me.

"Do you remember what you said to me earlier today?" I ask.

She nods against my chest.

"Can you say it again?"

"I love you, Ben."

I grin, feeling complete for the first time since I lost my family.

"I love you, too, Roxie."

EPILOGUE
ROXIE

I'm happy.

Six months later...

"That's the last of it."

I rub my dirty hands on my jeans as I watch Screamer carry in the last box. Today is moving day. The two of us talked a lot about where we wanted to live, and we agreed that staying at either clubhouse was off the table. Screamer respects the fact that I don't want to be surrounded by club business all the time, and I respect the fact that, just because he doesn't live with his club, doesn't mean he's not a part of it. Finding a house was a compromise we both knew we needed to make.

We closed on the ranch house a week ago, and both clubs have helped us pack and transport all of our belongings. They're all scattered throughout the house, putting together furniture, and generally doing whatever Screamer and I tell them to.

"Wait!" Rae says, running in behind him. "This fell out of your pocket."

She hands something small to Screamer, but I can't tell what it is because he turns away from me. Instead, I focus on my friend. It took longer than any of us would've liked, but about two months ago, she came to me and asked me to help her quit drinking. I happily agreed.

Mark has helped, too. Turns out, his mom is an alcoholic—sober for five years—so he's been the perfect support system for Rae. She's still grieving the loss of Saint, and probably always will. The important thing is that she's learning that it's okay, and despite how it feels sometimes, she's not alone.

"Thanks," Screamer mumbles.

"No problem."

Mark pokes his head through the front door. "You ready to go?" he asks Rae. "The meeting starts in a half hour."

He's been taking her to AA meetings several times a week, and it's helping for sure.

"Yep." Rae walks toward me and kisses my cheek. "Call me after you're settled in. We can get together for a girl's night."

"Count on it."

After they leave, Screamer turns to face me, a sheepish look on his face.

"What's up?"

"Nothing." His response is cagey, but I trust him.

Shrugging, I return to putting dishes away in the kitchen. "Wanna check on everyone? See if they're getting hungry. I can order some pizza."

It isn't until hours later that we're alone in our new house, both beyond exhausted. Screamer collapses onto the couch, pulling me into his lap.

"Are you happy?" he asks.

I look at him and smile. "You really don't know?"

"Humor me."

"Yes, I'm happy."

Scooting me to sit on the cushion, he slides to the floor and faces me. I watch as he reaches into his pocket and pulls out a black velvet box.

My hands fly to my mouth, and I suck in a breath. "W-what are you doing?"

Opening the box, he grins. "Roxie, I told myself I was going to wait longer, that I would give you more time to put some distance between what happened with Jace and moving forward. I had all these plans, and then this fell out of the box." He shrugs. "I'm taking it as a sign that enough time has passed, and I hope like hell that I'm not wrong. Roxie, sweetheart, will you marry me?"

Tears slide down my cheeks, and he brushes them away. Unable to form words, I nod.

"Yeah?" he asks.

"Y-yeah."

Screamer

Twenty-five years later...

"It's been a hell of a ride."

I clink my bottle against Crow's and stare out over the crowd. Everyone is here today. Each Soulless Kings MC brother, prospect, family member, and close friends. We've gathered to celebrate some of us retiring and the next generation taking the reins. Limitless Throttle MC also has a presence, as they do on all family gatherings because of my marriage to Roxie.

"How did we get here?" I ask, wanting to hear my pres's answer.

"Lots of pain and heartache," he says. "And lots of fucking love, brother."

"Yo, Dad?"

I turn to face my son, pride swelling in my chest as I watch him walk across the yard. "What's up?"

"Mom and Rosie want you to come inside for a minute," he says, not meeting my eyes.

"Everything okay?" I ask, suddenly worried. Benji doesn't avert his eyes... ever.

"Yeah, just... c'mon."

He whirls around and strides away, leaving me to follow.

"This can't be good," Crow says, walking beside me. "Roxie *and* Rosie summoning you? Fuck, when my wife and daughter team up, it always ends up fucking me somehow."

I laugh at his assessment because he's right. After Addison gave birth to their daughter, the amount of estrogen that Crow had to put up with about broke him. Don't get me wrong, he loves them and would die for them, but being hitched to the Chief of Police and captain of the cheer squad wasn't easy for him.

It was funny as hell for the rest of us though.

"What's going on?" Journey asks when we pass him, and he falls into step with us.

"Screamer was summoned," Crow says.

"Uh-oh. Both Rox and Rosie?"

"Yep," I mutter, getting more apprehensive by the second.

Journey and Wren never had children. Even

though Wren has a solid grip on her Dissociative Identity Disorder, and it's not genetic, they agreed that they didn't want to risk it. They've lived vicariously through the rest of us and our children. And to be honest, even if her different identities came out to play, I loved it when she watched Benji and Rosie when they were little.

"Heard your wife was looking for you," Ghost states, joining the ever-growing group of us.

"Fuckin' hell, word travels fast," I bark.

"You might not have lived here for over two decades," Ember says as she walks alongside Ghost. "But you know how things work. The gossip runs rampant."

I halt and turn to her. "Do you know what's going on?"

Her only response is to shrug. I trail my gaze from her to Ghost and the rest of them.

"What about all of you?" I demand.

"Nope."

"No."

"Course not."

I throw my hands up in the air, annoyed because it's clear that they know *exactly* what's going on.

"Is it time?" Poker asks, jogging in our direction.

"Fuck, you, too?"

I don't wait for him to respond before picking up my pace.

By the time I reach the back deck of the clubhouse, which was added about ten years ago as the kids started to get older, my heart is racing, and sweat trickles down my back.

"Roxie!" I shout when I step inside.

Fender, the asshole, steps in front of me. "Where are you going?"

"He was summoned by Roxie and Rosie," Crow answers before I can, and I groan.

"Oh, I know," Fender states. "But you have to go wait for them in the common room."

"Where are they?" I snarl.

Fender grins, and if he weren't such a good friend and the retired president of the Soulless Kings mother chapter, I'd clock him in the mouth.

"Follow me."

Benji slings his arm around my shoulder as we walk to the large room. "This is killing you, isn't it?"

"Just you wait, son," I say. "Someday, you're gonna have an old lady and children, and your life will no longer be your own."

"No fucking way," Benji says.

That causes laughter to break out through the crowd. I slowly turn around because the sound is deafening, and that's when I realize that every single person that was outside followed us in and is now crowded in the common room.

"Can someone please tell me what the fuck is goi—"

"Daddy, stop."

Rosie's sharp tone cuts through the laughter, and I spin around again to see her and her mother standing a few feet away.

"Honey, what's going on?" I ask her.

"I have an announcement to make," she says with a serene smile on her beautiful face.

Rosie is a carbon copy of her mom, and I wouldn't have it any other way. Well, all except for the pride and stubbornness. Those things cost me a lot of sleep while she was growing up.

I glance from her to Roxie. "Do you know what's going on?"

My wife grins. "I do."

"Jesus, Rosie, put me out of my misery," I plead, unable to take the secrecy a second longer.

Rosie closes the distance between us, and Roxie moves to stand at my side, sliding her arm through mine. Then my daughter hands me an envelope.

"Open it," she says.

I peel the flap back and slide out the photo that's inside. The weight of what I'm seeing hits me like a ton of bricks, and I lift my eyes to Rosie's.

"I'm gonna be a grandpa?"

"Yep. They'll be here in roughly seven months," she replies, rubbing her hands over her still flat belly.

"They?" Roxie asks, clearly not in on this part of the secret.

"Twins?" I breathe.

Rosie nods. "I'm hoping for a boy and a girl. It was great growing up with a brother, and I want that dynamic for my children."

"Aw, sis," Benji says, a teasing quality in his tone. "Love you."

"Love you, too, big brother."

My family of four settles into a hug, and cheers erupt in the room. For the next ten minutes, hugs, back slaps, and congratulatory fist bumps come from all around. Then a loud bang breaks up the commotion.

I look to my right where Fender, in all his grey-haired glory, is standing on the bar.

"I'd like to make a toast," he says, and again, cheers erupt. He continues when it quiets down. "A wise man," he begins, glancing at Royal, another retired brother from the mother chapter. "A wise man once told me something that's stuck with me. They say your life flashes before your eyes at the moment just before death. But ya know what?" He takes a deep breath. "They fucking lied."

Chuckles ripple through the crowd.

"They fucking lied," Fender repeats. "For the most part. What they got right is this... Life does flash before your eyes. It passes in a blur, and before you know it, you're reaching the end. Every flash makes up the memories of what I hope is a life well-lived. Royal's old lady has always captured those flashes with her camera. I've seen the pictures here on the walls of the clubhouse with the flashes in Marble Falls. Some of us need those pictures to remind us of the best parts of our lives."

He shifts his gaze to Rae, who stands with her hand in Mark's. They married a few years after Saint's death, and they have a son they named after her deceased husband. Little Saint isn't so little anymore and is actually married to Rosie. They married a few months after graduating high school because he was enlisting in the Army. It sucks that he's not here tonight, as he's finishing up his latest tour of duty, but I know he'll make an incredible father to my grandchildren.

"And to remind us of the worst parts," Fender continues solemnly. "Some of us have snapshots stored in our brains, forever in our grasp when we want to remember."

"Here, here!" Ghost shouts, lifting his glass.

"But then there's a third group of people, people

like all the club members here. We don't rely on pictures or the snapshot memories because we don't dwell on the past. We live in the moment. We live in the wind as it whips past us while we ride. We live in the present because yesterday is gone, and tomorrow isn't promised." Fender smiles sadly. "Fuck, we've all learned that the hard way. So," he jumps off the bar and walks to join me, Roxie, Rosie, and Benji. "Don't wait until you're about to die to let life flash before your eyes. Because whoever said that's how it works… They fucking lied."

IF YOU HAVEN'T READ THE ORIGINAL SOULLESS KINGS MC, CHECK OUT FENDER:

BOOK 1

Fender...

One night. That's all it takes for a person's life to forever be changed. One chaotic, unexpected, inevitable night and hundreds of bullets, two of them hitting my parents. I was born to be a Soulless King, born with sworn enemies and a loyal streak. Like a phoenix, I rise from the ash and vow to bring hell upon those responsible.

The problem with my vow is I'm not sure who is to blame. They tell me it's the temptress with emerald eyes, the one who used to share my bed. How can I be sure since she left without giving me the chance to find out the truth?

Now that she's back, she won't get away before I

ask my questions. But what if I don't like the answers?

Charlie...

As the princess of the Black Savages, I was raised to believe one thing: my club is my family, no matter what. But when they are responsible for shattering the life I created, I do the only thing I can. I run.

The thing about running is I can't do it forever. Life, past transgressions, tragedy... they hunt me down and drag me back, shoving me into the deep end of fate. And fate is a fickle bitch.

What if my fate is with *him*, the president of the Black Savages' sworn enemy?

PROLOGUE
FENDER

THEY SAY YOUR LIFE FLASHES BEFORE YOUR EYES AT THE MOMENT JUST BEFORE DEATH. THEY FUCKING LIED.

SLICK.

Wet.

Hot.

Perfect.

That's the only way to describe the pussy I'm buried in. Charlie moans, and the sound seems to echo around us in flawless rhythm with the headboard banging against the wall.

"That's it, baby," I growl as I reach between our bodies and rub circles over her clit with my thumb.

Charlie's eyes resemble an emerald in its purest form, and I'm lost, drowning in a sea of green. They widen and her pupils dilate the second her orgasm begins. Tingles race down my spine, and my body tenses as I join her.

We explode together, and the sounds we've created die down. My heart is pounding, and her breathing is labored. I roll off of her, carrying her with me and tucking her into my side.

"Holy shit, Fender."

"What?" I ask, a grin tugging at my lips. She always says the same thing after we fuck. Always.

"It gets better every—"

"Fender, get the fuck out here!"

The pounding on my door and the urgency in Piston's voice has me springing from the bed and grabbing my gun from the nightstand. That's when it registers. Gunshots, yelling, glass shattering.

"Fender! Now!" Piston's fist is an inch away from my face when I throw open the door. "Black Savages stormed the club. Get dressed and c'mon!"

I glance over my shoulder and see Charlie shoving her legs into her jeans. Her ass is encased in the black lace I pulled off her body with my teeth not a half hour ago. I hate to see her cover her flesh, but I can't think about that right now.

"Get in the fuckin' closet and don't come out. Not for anything." I grip her bicep and drag her to the door in the corner of the room, throw it open, and shove her in.

"Maybe I can talk to them. Maybe I—"

"No. They're past talking, and so am I." I crush her lips in a bruising kiss before shutting the door in her face.

I dress as quickly as I can and mentally prepare for what I'm about to face. Certainly nothing good. I make my way down the hall, my gun cocked and ready to blow away any Savage that gets in my path.

I just pray it's not Dyno. It would be great to take out the president of the Black Savages, but I can't do that to Charlie. I can't kill her dad.

I round the corner into the main room of the clubhouse and am shocked at the carnage. The floor is littered with broken liquor bottles and booze. There's also blood and bodies, and it's hard to tell which club the deceased belong to.

"Fender!"

I whirl toward the voice and see my father, his shirt soaked in blood, kneeling on the floor. My mother is cocooned in his arms, her body limp. Everything else melts away. The shouting, the gunfire, the mayhem. Cold calm washes over me as I walk toward my parents, ignoring the bullets whizzing past my head. Maybe I'd get lucky, and one would take me out, so I wouldn't have to face what I know is coming.

Time speeds up the closer I get. I drop to my knees. "Where are you hit?"

My father's stare is blank, empty. When he doesn't respond, I run my hands over his chest to determine if the blood is his or all from the hole I can now see in my mother's head. I don't allow myself to feel the loss. I can't afford to fall apart right now. My fingers hit a soft spot, a hole, on the left side of my father's chest. I rip the sleeves from his shirt and stuff the fabric in the hole to slow the bleeding. He hisses in pain, but that's his only reaction.

"Stay here," I shout at him, praying he hears what I'm saying. "I'll be back."

I lunge to my feet and storm into the middle of the room. I take a deep breath and find my first target. I point the gun and squeeze the trigger, not stopping until I've systematically taken out every Black Savage still standing, emptying the clip in the process.

"What the fuck was that?" Piston asks, walking through the bodies, kicking a few as he goes.

"Who'd we lose?" I survey the scene, trying to answer my own question.

"Stunner, Carbon, Phantom," Piston rubs his head, leaving a streak of blood. He's looking around, same as me. His head stops moving, and his gaze lands on something behind me. "Aw, fuck."

I slowly turn around, needing to see what he sees, and instantly regret it. My father is slumped over, both my parents are dead. It's fitting, I suppose. They lived for the club and died for it. It's what they would've wanted, to go out together in a blaze of glory.

Bang!

I pivot around at the gunshot, shocked to hear it because I thought the chaos was over. Charlie's standing there, her eyes wide, her arms straight, the gun in her hand. I follow her gaze to the man she just killed. Sharp, the Black Savages' Sergeant at Arms, is lying on the floor with a bullet hole between his eyes.

"He was gonna kill you," she mumbles.

"You need to leave," Piston demands. "You don't belong here."

My eyes dart back and forth between the woman I love and my best friend. He's absolutely right. She shouldn't be here. Especially now. But I don't have it in me to make her leave.

"Did you do this?" Joker shouts from behind Piston, directing the question at Charlie. "Precious Black Savages' princess coordinates Soulless Kings' massacre. Isn't spreading your legs enough to secure your place?"

Charlie's arms drop to her sides, and the gun clanks to the floor. She's staring at me, silently begging me to defend her, protect her from the lies my brother's spewing. Problem is, I can't. What if he's right?

"Get the fuck out!" Joker shouts, pointing toward the exit.

Charlie's eyes well with tears as she turns and runs out the front door. In my twenty-three years on this Earth, I've stared down the barrel of a gun more times than I can count, and it doesn't hold a candle to what I'm experiencing right now.

I was born to be a Soulless King, raised to be a ruthless, loyal motherfucker. None of that prepared me for this moment. Nothing could make losing so much any easier to swallow.

They say your life flashes before your eyes at the moment just before death. They fucking lied.

Your life flashes before your eyes at the moment you lose everything you live for.

ALSO BY ANDI RHODES

Broken Rebel Brotherhood

Broken Souls

Broken Innocence

Broken Boundaries

Broken Rebel Brotherhood: Next Generation

Broken Hearts

Broken Wings

Broken Mind

Bastards and Badges

Stark Revenge

Slade's Fall

Jett's Guard

Soulless Kings MC

Fender

Joker

Piston

Greaser

Riker

Trainwreck

Squirrel

Gibson

Flash

Royal

Satan's Legacy MC

Snow's Angel

Toga's Demons

Magic's Torment

Duck's Salvation

Dip's Flame

Devil's Handmaidens MC

Harlow's Gamble

Peppermint's Twist

Mama's Rules

Valhalla Rising MC

Viking

Inferno

Reaper

Mayhem Makers

Forever Savage

Saints Purgatory MC

Unholy Soul

Wrathful Malice

Grim's Hell

Shadowy Abyss

Rogue's Cross

Thorn's Vengeance

Spike's Perdition

Soulless Kings MC: Marble Falls, TX

Crow

Journey

Ghost

Poker

Screamer

Hellfire Hackers

Jezebel's Liberation

ABOUT THE AUTHOR

Andi Rhodes is an author whose passion is creating romance from chaos in all her books! She writes MC (motorcycle club) romance with a generous helping of suspense and doesn't shy away from the more difficult topics. Her books can be triggering for some so consider yourself warned. Andi also ensures each book ends with the couple getting their HEA! Most importantly, Andi is living her real life HEA with her husband and their boxers.